My Falling Down House

Jayne Joso

SEREN

Seren is the book imprint of
Poetry Wales Press Ltd
57 Nolton Street, Bridgend, Wales, CF31 3AE
www.serenbooks.com
Facebook: facebook.com/SerenBooks
Twitter: @SerenBooks

ISBNs
Pback – 978-1-78172-339-5
Ebook – 978-1-78172-340-1
Kindle – 978-1-78172-341-8

A CIP record for this title is available from the British Library.

The publisher acknowledges the financial assistance of the Welsh Books
Council.

Printed in the Czech Republic by Akcent Media Ltd.

My Falling Down House is a Recipient of **The Great Britain Sasakawa
Foundation Award** – given to a work of fiction or nonfiction which helps
to interpret modern Japan to the English-speaking world.

My Falling
Down House

For Greta Dowling Flaherty

'While we are young and without pain we not only
believe in eternal life, but have it.'
                                    Thomas Bernhard, Concrete

SUMMER

TOKYO

1.

Let me tell you who I am. My name is Tanaka, Takeo Tanaka.

My father says I'm an idealist, and that this will be my downfall. I disagree. Sometimes you just have to be patient and see how things play out.

As for the house, it's abandoned and dilapidated, but somehow I'm drawn back to it. It's a place I fell into about a year ago following a heavy night's drinking with co-workers. Back then my stay here was nothing more than an accident and only for one night. Strange to think that I ended up seeking the place out. But this is only temporary, and as soon as I recover I'll move on.

When I arrived here all I had with me was a box. Just a large ordinary cardboard box. I knew there was some of my stuff in there, I just didn't know what exactly, and so far I've lacked the curiosity to look inside.

A cat had joined me on my journey from the station. He was black and handsome looking, and I guessed he was still quite young – I remember how the heat kept everything weighted, our moves made in a sun and dust slow motion. When we reached the house he peeled off as though he had done his duty for the day.

Getting inside the house was tougher than I expected, and I knew I had to suck up my anxiety until I was safely in. I leant against the door to steady myself, the box making me clumsy. I glanced back to check I was alone. As long as no one slid open a door or drew back their shoji, all would be well. This wasn't my neighbourhood, and taking up residence, however temporarily, in a place that is not yours, is a tricky and potentially dangerous thing to do.

The door felt heavy and fragile and no longer fitted quite as it should. Clearly no one had done any work on the place. It was a falling down house, falling apart in stages, and I ought to treat it with care.

By now these traditional old houses were rare in Tokyo, most of them awaiting renovation or demolition, but mostly demolition because land prices are super high. So it was strange to find such a dwelling so close to the city, and in such bad condition; usually they are quickly removed, a pencil tower erected in their place or something very much larger. And it's hard to know exactly what criteria would save a place and what would line it up for the diggers. I couldn't guess how it would go with this one in the long run, but I hoped it would survive.

I snuck inside and shuffled the door shut. Finally, the world outside was gone. I could breathe again. I set the box down on the tatami.

The joints of the place creaked; the walls leaned whichever way seemed to ease them; the shoji was torn, yellow by now, and stained; and a purple-grey dust formed like tiny stalagmites all about the room. Clay dust sifted from the ceiling, a gentle reminder to take good care. I seemed to bow in recognition.

I sat a moment, the box settled next to me, and dusted my feet. For some reason that day I had not worn shoes and I realised now why the streets had felt so hot. I checked back around the entrance. No shoes there at all, just several pairs of slippers long since forgotten, coated in dust, and a single black umbrella. Cobwebs. I returned to the tatami and lay down by the box.

On my last birthday I turned twenty-five. And somewhere around that time I lost my job, my girlfriend, and my home. I wondered how it was possible to be quite that failed that soon.

I lay on the tatami I don't know how long, a sleepy honey-bee, my shoulders warm and soft, aware of how different this place seemed in bright white sunshine. A gentle breeze slipped through cracks and breaks in the windows making ripples in the shoji. The breeze caught a wind chime some-where – it startled me until I sensed what it was. I lay back down again and felt the sun pour in and over me, a yellow rain, and with it a wonderful heat. So intense I wanted to make a blanket of it, pull it all around me, and curl up inside. And I wanted to lie there that way a good long while nothing but nothing in my head.

When I woke my face was wet. My body dripped with sweat. I had taken off my clothes and laid them beside me.

I sat up and shuffled back on my heels and into the shad-ows as great slashes of light suddenly shot in, carving up the space. I watched as they formed a perfect golden geom-etry on the old and dusty wooden floor, up over steps, zigzagging across the tatami. Dust particles danced in the light. I noticed the breaks in the windows again, how damaged the place was. I wondered just how many quakes it had seen, and yet it was standing. Bent at the knees but standing.

The box seemed to have moved, or perhaps it was just that it didn't really seem to belong to me. And what did I need? Fleetingly, I thought about my cello. That day drinking with my co-workers I was so completely wasted that when I passed by a second-hand music shop, I wound up inside buying a cello. It's not the craziest thing I could have done, I used to play – what was crazy was that I bought one right then. I could barely stand, and I have no idea how I managed to get it safely to this place. When I woke my recollection of the night was all out of focus; I didn't even know where I was. I had to get to the office and the cello got left behind. It had to be here. I slid some doors back and hunted around. Nothing. I slid some more. Then more. It wasn't there. I stopped looking. Tense.

The cello didn't matter. The box didn't either. What I needed to do was to sit down and try to make sense of things. Too much had happened and I had to find a way to fix it. But right now my head was empty. Just space. A room without windows and nothing in it. It was all I could do to hope that a few days' rest would somehow put things right. Then I could return to the city and get on with it all. I began to wonder what my father would have said, Takeo Tanaka, you must face what has happened, and you must face yourself. But do not be afraid. I added the last sentence myself, that's not something he would say. In truth, I'll never know what he would say – I can't ever tell him.

I knew that one stroke of bad luck never broke a man, or even knocked him over. But several episodes – I might even call them events – that seemed a little more troublesome to negotiate, so I ought to handle the details with care. Until a few weeks ago I was gainfully if not that happily employed in the financial sector. It was a good job in all obvious respects, a very good job, and everything seemed to be headed in the right direction. I didn't question a thing. I already commanded a healthy salary, and my progression in the company seemed certain, assured. Alongside this, I had a girlfriend, Yumi, and the two of us lived together in a smart apartment in Setagaya, a smart part of town. It's hard to stomach that losing one thing could possibly lead to losing it all, but that's what happened. Perhaps I was arrogant. Or simply naive. But I thought I had a job for life, a place to call home.

I have to get some water. And I should wash.

For a while I managed to sleep at my old office. Shizuka was a cleaner there, she was quite young, younger than me at least, and she would help me hide out. It was a system that evolved when Yumi and I fell out from time to time. When everyone else had left for the day, I would make a kind of nest under my desk. I had a box and Shizuka brought me a blanket. Box Man, she would call me. You are the Box Man, and she would laugh warmly. Then she would head home and return in the early hours, waking me before anyone else arrived. This was just about manageable as long as I still worked there. My suit would get crumpled but really that was the worst of it. I remember I developed some skill in box sleeping, even taking pride in fitting into the box quite so neatly. Human origami, the foldaway man. But sneaking in and out of the place was much harder to get away with once I lost my job, and I couldn't risk being the cause of Shizuka losing hers.

Strange to think that this series of events now positioned me as little more than a criminal. But that's how it looked. My life had become too slippery and, like a soft ball of sweet, sticky rice, once it fell it simply gathered more and more mess. A man, when he falls, first becomes a box man, and next a sticky ball of rice. It's not a good way for things to go.

There had been an economic downturn, a crisis, and like many I was surplus to requirements. My girlfriend had no interest in a man without an income, and lacked the patience to wait while I found something new. Bills mounted and drained my account. Yumi took on the apartment on her own, and I moved out. I did not live in Setagaya anymore, and whatever was in the box was clearly the last of my possessions. A few belongings chosen by Yumi. My world: the contents of a single box.

2.

Somewhere it is detailed how many days a man might last without food and in what condition his mind could find itself. If the man has also experienced trauma the symptoms might be exacerbated and include hallucinations, both visual and auditory. I read about a soldier, long after a war was over, wandering in a forest in just such a state. I cannot remember the outcome.

During the night I grew feverish and woke sensing that someone else or something else was in here. I sat up and held my breath. Sand shivered from the wall behind me. I kept myself firmly in the darkest spot, so that if there was something it would not see me. My hands curled into fists. The air unsettled, I could hear and feel my breathing. Something moved above my head. I feared the ceiling giving way and braced myself. I crouched down, wrapping my head in my arms like an ape. Whatever it was landed heavily but moved about the room with ease. If I had to, I would fight. The box shifted on the tatami, then turned over. I came to my feet and raised my fists. The walls moaned and shifted in the shadows. The paper shoji teased me, rippling in the dark; menacing images eased themselves up and over the walls, lurching above me. Lunging, retreating, shivering their menace. The wind chime tinkled softly and fell silent. Everywhere, silent. Perhaps it was the cat.

I breathed, and found myself kneeling, my head lowered to the floor. If there was something, it had gone now. And perhaps I had been dreaming.

When eventually I raised my head I noticed something that I had not seen before, in the alcove. A cello. My cello. Laid upon its side, like a woman sleeping. Quickly, I inched my way over the tatami close to the ground. I touched its dusty surface. Even in the dark I was sure of what it was. Kneeling, I raised it upright, then I shuffled forward gently and centred it in the alcove where I guessed it had been standing. I released my grip and hoped it would not fall again.

After a moment I moved back to the upturned box, and wondered why a cat would find it interesting. I brushed my foot lightly over the contents, but there was nothing there that mattered, just clothes it seemed. I put them back, closed the lid, and pushed the box aside again.

If I was going to stay in this place a few nights longer, I had to stop taking fright so easily. When I came here a year ago it was completely dark and I was drunk. I couldn't have described it on the inside save for the obvious; I just recalled a sense of being perfectly at ease. All I needed was a place to hide out and rest until I was myself again, just a roof over my head, a little food if I could find some, but really nothing more. Even without food I would be fine in a few more days. I had come here because I was drawn to the place, there was a feel for nature here, a sense of a slow and simple way of living. A forgotten way of living. There was nothing here to harm me. Earth, wood, sand and stone, and tatami beneath my feet. And now I had the cello. This house was on my side.

3.

It didn't sit easy with me to stay some place (no matter how dilapidated) that wasn't mine and for which I paid no rent. I decided that as long as I was here I would make myself useful and fix what I could. The work would distract me, and in a day or two my mind would calm and I would figure things out – and I saw no reason not to make a few repairs and make the place more habitable. I would make notes and then fix what I could. I just needed to be careful that I wasn't seen or heard. I had already been too casual when searching for the cello, slamming a door, snapping it hard into its frame. With that in mind, and until I was sure if anyone spied upon the place, I decided to start my activities at night.

So far I had discovered very little about the house, save for the toilet and a running tap allowing me to drink and wash. Now I would scope the place out and start to get acquainted with the house in full.

Determined not to draw attention to myself I kept for the moment to the floor, moving about mostly on my hands and knees, sometimes hands and feet. It was quite an efficient method; I didn't know where there would be windows or possibly even breaks in the walls (perhaps where the cat had made its entry), but it was imperative that I was not found out. I moved from space to space taking in what I could, my sight still adjusting to the dark. But I quickly got a sense of its vastness on the inside, really it was huge, and it struck me that this was quite a trick since its narrow facade on the street gave the impression of a very much smaller place. I liked this. A house of great proportions disguised as something entirely modest. A big house in a small house.

I took a rest and thought back to my office and the box dwelling. I tried to recall its dimensions. Truly, if Shizuka had not helped me at certain points, I could so easily have joined the ranks of the homeless. A box in an office is something quite different from a box in the street. A shiver ran across my back.

Quickly I settled myself back to exploring, struck by the strong sense of nature inside the place. Clay, wood, straw and stone. I could smell the smoke-blackened timbers. I put my hands inside the broken walls and touched bamboo, I rolled around on dark earth floors and tatami, and wrapped myself in rough, worn cloth. As morning came, impenetrable

17

shadows formed themselves all around me, long and wide, deep and narrow, and then were gone. The place changing right before me as the light filtered in. From the floor I lay and watched a good long while. A nice position. It was getting lighter, and I had been awake the whole night through.

I had discovered that the place also had an upstairs level, another trick hidden from the street from which I'd entered, but I would save it for another day. And from my current position I could see, through the haze of emerging sunlight and a break in the window, the outline of buildings on the other side, and perhaps a garden. Close by it was overgrown. I didn't mind at all, it offered some privacy, but when the time seemed right I would explore that side more closely.

Of my findings so far a stove, cooking pots, and a sack of rice, a huge sack of rice – a good six months' supply – had been my greatest treasures. The rice seemed old, but I would eat it nonetheless. Even so I did not eat straightaway, some-how I was sated by the mere idea of food. I had gone hungry some days but was not certain at all how many; or perhaps it was not that the idea sated me but simply that my energy was spent. I took a handful of the dry grains, and watched them fall through my fingers. My forearms and knees were sore from crawling, I dripped water over them. Sweating again, I laid myself down and wiped away my tears. I would rest awhile, and then I would cook.

Nestling on the tatami Cat is here. I observe Cello in the distance and she appears to be content. Propped up comfortably in the centre of the alcove, in a space all her own – and perhaps it is even a stage of her own where later she might perform. For now it seems all parties are restful and happy simply to sleep in the sun and in the shadows.

4.

My adjustment to nocturnal life was going well. As night fell I was always glad of the work ahead and in the mornings I was generally so exhausted I easily slept the daylight hours through. The only thing that suggested the daytime sleeps were possibly a mistake was the sheer number of mosquito bites printed over my skin. Always so hot, I never thought to cover up. It was hard to imagine that my blood offered anything nourishing on a diet of old rice, but these small creatures seemed certain it was for sharing. I lay awake awhile and watched them fly above me as though heavy and drunk, moving about in a slow and seemingly ordered formation, synchronised against a hazy, soupy sun.

I settled my thoughts on the lampshade above me. Paper and bamboo, a small imitation of the walls of wood and paper inside this place. Walls within walls. Holes within holes. I liked this place. If I had to I could happily stay here some time. I bathed and drank some water.

When I returned from bathing Cat had arrived. I lay on the tatami a moment and he padded about, making fun with his paws in my long wet hair. I sat up sharply and shook out the water. The spray startled him. I laughed and he withdrew, turning then to show me his back. When I looked again he had moved, and settling himself close to the box he eyed me as though suggesting I should open it.

I pulled it near and rummaged through. Truly there was nothing there I could not live without. By now it staggered me to realise just how much junk I had filled my life with. Always spending. Yumi, always spending. And then I found something, something Yumi would not have known the meaning of, for if she had she would certainly have kept it. My insect box. It was actually a box to keep letters in, an old-fashioned lacquer box given to me by my uncle as a child, but since I never received letters I had designated it my insect box. It didn't hold together quite as well as it should and so I tied it with a thin strip of silk, something stolen from my mother's sewing box. A green silk strip around an old battered box. When I was small I had planned to keep examples of different species of insect in the box as though I was a great explorer. But when it came to it I couldn't do it. Storing up little dead bodies lined up in rows, ultimately I didn't get it. But despite not receiving letters and not wanting to store up the dead, I always managed to make use of it. And a while back it was where I kept my gambling stash. I bet on the horses mostly, sometimes pachinko or mah-jong, but mainly horses. And since declaring my winnings meant admitting to gambling, I simply hid the cash away, and now inside this battered box lay a not inconsiderable sum.

I never cared about the money, but the gambling gave me a buzz. Something I never got from my job. All the bank ever did was chew up my soul. Strange to think this gambling hoard might just put things right. It could help me pay my way somewhere. An entire stack of notes. Big ones. I flicked through them. Their smell lifted off them. I patted them down again, laying them back in the box. If I was careful, this money would keep me quite some while.

I could start over. But then that thought filled me with anguish. I can't explain. Perhaps a jolt I hadn't anticipated, and wasn't quite ready for. Start over? This was far from me. But it had to be good, and perhaps it was not *too* far, and so, as soon as I felt able, I could leave this place, take up some modest residence so as to eke out the funds, and later, after I'd found a job, I could find a smart place again. That's how it would go. And step by step I would ease my way back into society.

I moved into the sunshine to feel its warmth on my face. What grand plans suddenly.

It had been a comfort to find I still had uncle's box. Gently I retied the ribbon, and returned it to the cardboard box.

5.

As the nights progressed a routine began to shape itself. I would go about my work, checking out each room, each space, assessing the damage, and noting things I might make use of. Sometimes Cat accompanied me, and sometimes I felt his presence on the upper floor as he padded about, teasing the more fragile timbers. Shivers of dust and sand would fall from the ceiling, but so far nothing more. But later, when I tried to sleep, my concern would grow that building inspectors might come here at any moment, or the owners of the dwelling, or, at extreme moments of anxiety, the police armed with sticks and batons. It was hard to gauge whether anyone ever checked on the house and I wondered if it was possible that there really were no eyes upon the place. I could only hope this was the case for it seemed certain now that I could not continue my work only at night-time. The strain on my sight was too great, and whilst I'd made some progress, there were real limitations as to what I could achieve only in darkness and the early half-light.

The project I worked on had really grown now and entirely by itself. Having discovered the sheer scale of the place it was obvious that the work was going to be very much more than I'd anticipated. I didn't mind. I was glad of it. But it was clear that I would need to become more thoroughly acquainted with the place before I could begin any greater repairs. I was also aware of my good fortune in arriving after the rainy season, but for sure the rains would come again, and if I was to stay here longer the place would have to be shored up.

I needed a full and detailed ground plan, careful notes and mapping, and an inventory of everything I found. Everything needed to be clear and precise, and if all of this required my staying here some extra days, then that's what I would do.

In many ways my progress seemed incredibly slow. I still hadn't ventured to the floor above, and still hadn't made it out into the garden, but I would get there. The greatest impediment was the sheer level of dilapidation. I'd lost count of the times I'd smashed my head, and as much as I could bear these minor collisions, if I wasn't careful it was only a matter of time before I actually dislodged some essential part of the building and then the damage to the house might prove catastrophic, and for me could signal the end. There was really no choice but to move about the place at a snail's pace and to attempt the work with care. If anyone came here, I had no idea what official powers they would have, but I would simply have to face them when it happened. Fear of the dark, fear of the light. Fear of the outside, and fear of what comes in. It does no good to let thoughts like that take hold.

6.

Aware that it was quite a step to move about the place in daylight I decided to maintain a state of high alert. Mindful not to draw attention to myself, I should be nothing more than a shadow here, that if anyone were to notice something strange behind a window, they would take it for the impression of a man but not a man himself, permitting themselves to accept what they see as nothing more than an illusion, a strange configuration. With this in mind I would stay as close to the walls as possible and particularly to any existing shadows. The perfect silent ninja.

I sat awhile with Cello and a bowl of rice to which I had added some water achieving a kind of poor man's porridge. It didn't taste good but I was indifferent to it somehow, excited by the next stage in my plans, eager to move things on.

So far I had made my notes on rough scraps of paper now hardly legible. What I scribbled in the dark often made no sense when I looked at it later in the light, and dust and moisture would mix and blur the lines I drew. This time I would draw up a clear and accurate plan with notes detailing every last aspect of the place, and since it would be easier to see, I could take care to keep the text clean and dry. By now I had found paper in various forms: scrolls, rolls, loose sheets and set in notebooks. I might use some of the fresh shoji paper I had found for larger scale drawings, I liked its texture; and if my notes were sufficient I would compile a journal. I might even execute some drawings as though conceiving a large and elaborate scroll. And since there was no one here to see it, I would call it art. I had also found a room crammed with cardboard boxes, collapsed down and piled up high, discarded and forgotten, but if possible, I would also put these to use. It might even prove helpful to create some models of the space here. I had been a fool to think I might have accomplished all of this work myself. The greater part of the repairs were clearly beyond me, but if I could put together a detailed record then this would surely help some expert when the real work of renovation began; and if it was good enough, it might also serve as part of an argument for renovation over demolition. And if any part of this place should fall whilst I was here, then it would help them to know what lay beneath the wreckage, what stood here before. So, it was decided, I would sketch and I would write.

I needed to see this house from every angle, every recess, every crevice, every shadow; saturated in light, in deepest darkness and every shade in between. And I would see it with heart and soul and capture all the things that eyes alone would surely miss. I would touch and feel this dwelling with every single part of me, my hands upon its skin, my chest against its walls.

A man falls in love with a house. So it goes.

7.

Something is wrong. It is not always Cat that moves about above my head. And I can no longer attribute the sounds to the timbers merely contracting and relaxing with the change in temperature as day and night move on. I listen closely. I am well attuned to the sounds in this place and know what each of them is. But the sounds that filter from the upper level are new sounds and they menace me. I have no weapon. Just the strength in my arms.

Afraid now, I will stay in the room I sleep in, close to Cello. I have tried to busy myself making notes, but find myself distracted. Sometimes the sounds seep away. But then they return and still I cannot name them. Does someone come here? And leave again? Do they spy on me? Gathering evidence, noting my moves, my desperate way of living? Why don't they make themselves known to me? Do they plan to attack me? I sit in the dark here waiting, knowing that at some point someone will come. And when they do I will not know who they are and I don't know what they'll do. What powers they will have.

Again the sounds. And then the quiet. Perhaps they choose their moment. Perhaps they seek to undermine me first with mind games and with torment. Perhaps a shapeshifter comes here. Is that the case?

I inch my way in silence to the cardboard box and take out the smaller lacquer box and make my way as quietly as possible to the door. All the while taking care to keep myself close to the ground, mindful of my moves. I should leave and find a better place, a safer, cleaner place. Pay my way somewhere, raise my head again. All in all, that would be for the best.

My hands shake. I struggle to control them. Unwashed the last days, I itch, and my limbs are cold. Perspiration slips down my back. I feel my way to standing but it's difficult, I have been crouched too long. I touch the door. It doesn't open and I can't find my strength. I reach back into the darkness of the room and I tremble. The sounds come again and I am so afraid. Around and around my head, the noises come. How is it possible to fear the outside more than this? I slip to the earthen floor, the silk-tied box clutched to my belly. My mouth lies open as though I would scream, and nothing but nothing comes, and without a sound my eyes let slip a few fat tears, and it is all I can do to sit and watch as they fall and pool upon my knees.

I remember a choking sensation, then nothing more.

Long after the sounds had gone I must have made my way back to the tatami, but in truth I do not remember the moves; and somehow, perhaps simply from exhaustion, I have slept. I am filthy from crawling, and hungry to a level that is now hard to gauge. There are pains in many parts of me, but especially my head. I cannot measure if that is also just a symptom of hunger; but perhaps my head was struck, or I fell down? What to make of it? What to do? Afraid of all the other rooms, I have decided that I should continue to keep myself in this one. An oasis from where I can see Cello. And I should maintain my position in the very darkest spot, so that no one hears or sees me. So full of fear, I would have to manage without the rice just now.

I hoped that Cat would come.

8.

I seem to have slept and slept again, and each time I woke I sensed that I had been dreaming, imagining some treacherous shapeshifter come here to plague me. Arriving at this house in some innocent form, perhaps some familiar human form that draws no attention to itself, but once inside, changing, choosing its prey and toying with sounds that unsettle the mind, starving the resting of their sleep, or filling the sleeping head with torment. This cannot be real though, and shapeshifters – only the stuff of folklore used to frighten us as children, to make us behave, to make us lie still. They are not real. *They are not real.*

Choosing my moment, I crept to the stove and finally set some rice to cook. I crouched down low on the floor, waiting as the steam rose above, hoping that nothing and no one would come.

Poor food, excessive heat, and unsettled sleep will certainly alter a man's state of mind. And being holed up like this is not healthy. I could almost hear my mother and aunt, their words filtering softly as though through the wind chime. Fresh air and exercise, Takeo, that's what you need. And thirty ingredients, each and every day. The mind and the body, that's what you need, Takeo, each and every day.

As a boy I would sit and studiously count the number of things that passed my lips each day. But I never went short. No need for worry. Beans and herbs and root vegetables, mountain vegetables in springtime (which I would gather with my cousins), rice and tofu, miso, fish and meat, and so many kinds of seaweed and fruit. Mushrooms and pickles. All in abundance these things danced across my palate, filled my greedy belly, and no doubt nourished me well. But now, how my belly cries out. And what I would give for a dish, *a huge great dish*, of broiled eel with an excellent teriyaki sauce. *Oh, god!*

But it's no good to do this. And I have to stop or thoughts of food will be the end of me. I have rice, I have water. Thirty ingredients – at present, I have just two. The rice alone will last many months, but it is not enough to maintain good health. I have to find greater nourishment soon or these dark dreams might never leave me.

9.

Without the courage to leave there was no easy answer as to what this greater nourishment could be or how I might come by it, and this spawned afresh the menace of anxiety. Terrifying thoughts soon plagued my head, awake as in sleep. Gnawing away at every part of me. Chomping, pecking, biting. Grinding up my soul. And the sounds, *the sounds* ... still they made their prey of me. *So go ahead! Gnaw away, grind up my soul, tear my senses from the tree, and soon I will be done with!* But let it be over.

In vain, I hoped these corrosive attacks might at least trigger something. Anything! An acceleration of thought or emotion, some spontaneous act that could somehow lead somewhere, a rupture, an idea, at least some slight shift, *anything ... anything at all!* But still, nothing useful in my head. I took up my notes, but my stomach ached from being endlessly filled with nothing but fetid old rice, and more recently eating nothing at all caused its own kind of pain; and I knew, deep down, that I had to act before I truly grew too weak, before I truly lost my mind.

Soon, I scribbled in the corner of my notes, *soon...*

Moving to a different spot I wondered where Cat might be. I hoped that he was safe. I hoped that he had food. I could hear the cicada outside. What a noise they make. The males, as though singing, perhaps even crying, for love, for sex. And I could so easily cry that way. When I lie awake in the night heat, at times my body takes on a certain kind of stress. No love making, no one to reach out to, no one here at all. Not a hand to hold, no one to talk to. It's difficult to capture the feeling. A longing. A loneliness. Just feelings, and I try to ignore them. But the more my mind settles on the cicada, their noise burrowing deep inside my skull, the more I'm afraid I will become one. Screeching and screeching, lying here in this old wooden house all alone.

I think of those bugs waiting there for years, deep, so deep underground. Suddenly they emerge out into the world. Offered only a few brief days of life, in some cases only hours, for they might quickly find themselves made prey – it's really never good to be a bug, not any kind of bug, I'm sure of it, but how can they bear so much stress? And now as I close my eyes, vividly I picture myself as one of them. All that darkness. Buried below ground those long years. Then rising up, seeing the sky for the very first time, and daylight. *Bright, white, daylight.* Piercing through their five mad eyes. Then the tension ahead – the pressure to mate, and just a few meagre grains of life opening up, and time compressed to encompass the narrowest set of possibilities. Moments zipping past with such extreme acceleration you cannot even imagine. How would you even permit yourself to waste the time on breathing? I see how it could be, I would emerge just like them, almost possessed. So full of intensity, of passion and yearning, and my god, just like each one of them all I would want is to make love, and to make love like crazy. If someone would have me, that's what I would wish.

A man when he falls, first becomes a box man, and then a sticky ball of rice; after this, he is an insect. I see how it goes. I almost find it amusing. But I had better be mindful, it seems there may be few positions left.

Distantly, I sense my father calling, his voice warm and round, Takeo! Before you fall, use a stick. You are right, Father, but it's too late. I have fallen down and down, and just now the walls around me close in, and lined with nothing but loose soil it is difficult to clamber out. But I will do it, Father, I will find a way back – moving only downwards is not the way to go. I see that.

10.

Still, I have not slept well, and still I have not settled on how I might find better food, and so the dreams continue to devour me.

In the last dream I saw Yumi. It was the day we parted. I'd stayed away from our apartment for a couple of nights and hoped that might just be enough, usually it was. We had been together for three years, there was a rhythm to it all. She'd get mad, I'd stay away, after a day or two I'd come back home. And for a good long while things were sweet again. But it was different this time. I climbed the steps to our apartment. My anxiety increasing with every step. At the door instinctively I bowed my head – eye contact can sometimes be too complicated. Afraid to risk anything, I pressed the buzzer but kept looking at the ground. Lightly I skimmed the sole of my shoe across the concrete floor. After a few long moments Yumi opened the door. She didn't speak at all, instead she turned back into the apartment and collected up a box placed just inside. It seemed this had been planned. Still avoiding looking up, I observed the manoeuvre from the lower legs down – feet and ankles, the hem of her skirt. When she had the box steady, her feet moved my way again so that she was facing me. It was as though she was automated, and she pushed the box determinedly from her chest into mine, forcing me to raise my hands and capture it. I looked at her straight on now and was about to speak, but the words? Somehow they didn't find my voice. Yumi had a wide piece of tape pressed hard across her face. A wide, red, slightly crinkled rectangle that covered over her mouth completely. The edges raw and uneven, pinching in half her cheeks to either side. A red slash where her mouth should have been. You had to stare, it was disturbing, especially so close, and I was worried; the whole scene ... strange and messed up. I think I would have tried to pull it off and release her, but my hands were firmly gripped to the box, stuck somehow; and though it sounds completely weak, I was nervous. I didn't think she had been taken captive, but I quickly scanned the room from where I stood. There didn't appear to be anyone else around, no one lurking in the background, no scent or feel of anything untoward, and the rest of her body looked entirely free, except perhaps for the eyes. Her eyes looked a little rounder than I remembered. They were fixed in a stare – I had never experienced anything like this. She switched her focus to the box. I did the same. There was a note attached, but before I could take hold of it, I received a hard shove and was ejected from the doorway. I almost fell. The door slammed.

I set the box down, sat on the step close by and read Yumi's note. It told me in no uncertain terms what she had already yelled to my face several days earlier, it was over, I was useless, adding now that she never wanted to speak to me again. Only this last part had already been made clear. Bright red tape clear.

I remember almost waking from that dream, I rolled around sweating, trying to climb out of it, and I heard the cicada beside me forcing away the earth in their attempts to set themselves free, but I fell back, and fell back into dreaming, and was made to enter this street again. I had the box with me. Forever fixed to my hands, my fingers gripping tightly. And I was made to walk this same route over, and over. And each time I journeyed down the street the box got heavier, the sun became more blinding, the atmosphere more menacing. And I saw myself in the distance, in miniature, trying to make it down the street, box in my arms, nothing on my feet, sun in my eyes; willing myself, just willing myself, not to be seen. This played itself out in endless repetition, and each time I arrived at the falling down house and tried to make my way in, I was thrust back to the top of the street with a hit to the chest, and had to make way again, over and over, and always carrying the box. And with each repeat the stress increased, for someone would see me, they would notice the man, they would notice the man and wonder at his repeated journeys. They would see what place he entered, and they would want to know the reason why. I have no business here. No business here at all. Someone will come. Perhaps the police, wanting to investigate, already on their way. Or a team of psychiatrists keen to unpack my brain. What kind of man am I? What am I doing here? Occupying such a run-down dwelling, what kind of person does that? And falling down or not, I have no right at all to be here, I stay both without permission and without payment. No sir, I did not even ask. No, I do not have a key. I broke in, I suppose, but the door, it was not locked. And my appearance? I was here some long months before in a suit, in a state of complete drunkenness, and now in a state of general disarray, possibly approaching the appearance of the homeless and the dispossessed. A man who could not easily be vouched for, not locally at least, for not a soul would know me hereabouts; and no sir, I possess no ID, not a single thing to name me. And the extreme changes in my appearance – these are in fact exactly the kinds of things which make people take notice. How peculiar my behaviour will seem, a young man, his hair grown long, a box in his hands, no shoes upon his feet.

Having lost so much I have almost come to feel I have no right even to exist, and perhaps I don't. I search for words to explain why I am here, and who I am, but they do not come, and I can no longer be sure that my behaviour is not strange, for I feel myself grown nervous. The vagrant, the illegal immigrant, what stress they must have. I think about my box.

Again, I am made to press on down the street. I force my head upwards, trying to give the appearance of casual confidence, of nonchalance. But each time it gets harder. At the door, I wait cautiously, I glance over my shoulder. I push at the door. But this time, *this time*, someone walks by, a man, and so I cannot enter. I move my head to avoid his gaze. I might have dropped something or perhaps I am simply waiting for someone. I keep still and hope he will think nothing more of it and simply move along. But he does not move and the waiting just gets longer. The box is heavy. My breathing short. My temper rises. Why doesn't he just go away? Carry on about his business. His own business. What does he want from me? And now another follows on behind him and someone else leaves their dwelling. And all the while the box gets heavier. Pain begins to rise in my legs and in my back. Why is this place suddenly so busy? What do they want with me? Agitated. My temper truly failing now, I almost lash out. But I know I have to find a lighter frame of mind. I stand motionless and pretend to myself that I am not there. I take the decision to remove my mind from my body, for no one can strike up conversation with only my shell. And if I do not occupy my body then I cannot be accused. For you surely cannot accuse someone if they are not fully present. And standing before the door, in my mind I feel myself begging: *just let me slip inside this place and let me breathe again. I am just a young man!*

And then I woke.

11.

It was daylight. I looked at my body, how thin it had become. I thought about food.

Cat arrived. He dropped something at my feet. A partially masticated corpse. I turned away. Tried to focus my thoughts.

Slowly I came to my feet. There were no sounds just now that I did not know. Nothing I did not recognise. Nothing here to harm me. I would wash.

I thought of Shizuka and wondered how she was doing. I hoped she had not lost her job. But cleaning is essential, and banking is not. She would probably be alright. Still, I wished her something better.

I turned the tap, but the water was no longer refreshing. My skin had grown sensitive, and I experienced the cold water like something that would burn me. The red marks seemed to attest to that. I could not trust it. I turned off the tap and patted my skin.

By now my dreams were becoming so lucid, they seemed to meld with reality so cleanly that at times I was no longer confident which were true conscious moments and which were dreams, phantoms. For several hours I would inhabit a stream of thoughts only finally to wake up fully and realise that the moments or hours before belonged to a dream-scape and my unconscious self. I was disturbed by this and could only find comfort in the fact that although there was sometimes a delay in my awareness, I did still retain the capacity to distinguish between the two states. I *could* still make out what was real. But for how much longer? I couldn't entertain the idea that I might lose this faculty altogether, and so I tried actively to cultivate my mental activity during the periods when I was certain I was conscious. Always taking notes, updating the inventory, adding in anything I deemed essential.

I was especially pleased by all the boxes I had found, and

had by now named the room in which they lay *the box room*. It seemed appropriate to name each room, define its function, its personality. And the work I was doing was useful. But as each clear moment visited me, thoughts of my declining health and my ability to stay aware keenly fed my anguished state. I had to find food. Soon, I wrote again, *soon…*

I began to tease myself, summoning up memories of summer picnics and feasting at New Year. For when a man lacks water, that is all he will think of. The hunger was becoming quite paralysing but I needed to push myself into moving, into finding something more. I thought that if I could achieve a state of *absolute* hunger, provoked by fantasies of tasting, of savouring, and the remembrance of fullness, that this might just animate me, force me into action, into overriding all other fears, that I find myself some better food. And so I allowed the thoughts to run.

I thought of my time as a box man and how Shizuka would sometimes stop by late into the evening with a small set of containers of wonderful spicy food. Once she brought my favourite dish, *yukhoe*. Beautiful fresh raw beef; a raw egg yolk, shining golden, settled in the centre, soon beaten in with the smallest drop of sesame oil and some true hot seasoning. That would be the perfect nourishment right now. In the matter of taste, even a little kimchi would suffice, though it would not fill me nor build my strength. But I would like at least to taste a little kimchi. Kimchi, and an ice-cold summer beer. Shizuka was addicted to Korean food, I never saw her eat anything else, and right now I would give anything for a few of those delicious dishes, perhaps something with garlic.

And now I smell something. Do I imagine it? I imagine it. For sure, I do. But this is a food I know too well, and it is real. It must be real. Its flavour hopping on the breeze, a newly fractured window permitting its entrance. I crane my neck and touch my face, wondering if some residue might be captured there. I lick my fingertips. Something? It's hard to tell. I breathe it in again. It is familiar, appetising, and though it is subtle, my nose tells me it is something tasty. Tasty and real. And it is weaving its way inside this place in a very tantalising manner. Miso. It is miso. *And how I have missed you.* The winds favour me and the flavour dances in here just now from the garden side. I follow my nose and must look over there more closely.

I wipe a window.

Travelling in a straight line across the way there is a house whose dimensions seem to match, I would almost say mirror, those of this decayed dwelling – though the one over there appears to be in pristine condition. To the right, joining both the perfect dwelling and my own, is what exactly? A temple? I crane my neck further, I cannot see as clearly as I would like to, but it is a temple. Must be.

All in all, it would appear that there is an inner courtyard, surrounded by four buildings. These appear to be linked. This suggests the temple as the starting point, and implies that the three other structures, including the house I dwell in, belong in some way to the temple itself. In the centre there is the garden, and this is very neat, quite unlike the area close to this house where it is heavily overgrown. From here I can make out a small pond, tall slender clusters of bamboo, trees, and moss, a great deal of moss, and stones of various sizes, each of them entirely smooth. And now I see someone. An old man peers in my direction. For the moment he does not seem to see me. Perhaps he is so old that he cannot focus well enough to find my shape behind the glass. But I had better keep still. His face looks gentle. His hair is white, his beard, short and wispy. His eyes are tired but kind and twinkling. The light changes, and he has gone. He had a look of my grandfather about him. No matter. And now there's someone else, but they are further away and I cannot make them out so well. An old woman perhaps? Seems that way. She is bent over as she moves, as though afraid to occupy the upper space, her back almost a table-top. Perhaps this is a local woman come to leave an offering at the temple, or perhaps she is one of the staff there. Would that she would fetch me some miso soup and some other great dishes to accompany it.

It looks so calm, almost serene out there. Quite different from the banal street life on the other side. I like it much better.

The old woman has gone, but now another sweeps the steps up to the temple entrance. A man is tending the broad but simple garden. I smell incense. A second man has joined him, a younger man. A woman arrives carrying foodstuff, fruit or so, an offering I expect. A child follows on behind her. They enter the temple. Where do they all come from? It is a somewhat ethereal experience to stand and watch this simple activity. There is a pervading sense of gentle continuity as each person moves about the space and goes about their daily chores with ease. Someone leaves the temple now, a monk. Bows are exchanged. I am calmed by the atmosphere of tranquillity I see, but I had better move or someone will certainly catch my shape at the window.

The slightly salty taste of miso lifts and hovers in the air, and I am decided. When the light has gone, I will make my move.

12.

The sun has played with me today; waiting for the light to fade never took so long. I can't stand it, and I simply won't go on like this. I must eat. I can only hope that no one sees me. I try the door on this side and realise it is the first time I have done so. I must be cautious that it does not make a deal of noise. So many leaves inside this place, all dry and crisp, blown in on some forgotten autumn, thick with dust. I had better sweep them further in for if they blow outside and into the temple garden I will arrive out there like some bizarre phantom pushing on the seasons long before their time.

I brush them up in haste. All done. A mountain of dust and dirt-filled leaves now stands inside my room. Mount Fuji in an autumn coat.

At the door again, I gather myself. My heart lies in my mouth and I can hardly breathe. I step out. The light drops. I take a breath. The moon is out. My courage rises.

Poorly dressed with nothing on my feet, my skin unwashed some days, I will have the appearance of a beggar. No matter.

In my hometown in the mountains, the temple doors always went unlocked, and the same was true of many houses, but I doubt that will be the case on the outskirts of the city. I might find trouble. I must be swift and silent and firm in this endeavour. I don't have a plan; I am simply driven to satisfy this hunger. I make the moves up as I go. And it will work, for it has to, I must eat now or I will be driven insane.

I hear voices. I shiver and crouch down low and it grows quiet. I keep still awhile. I take a step and stop again. Breathing deeply. Not sure whether to move or not. I stay put a moment longer. The moss feels good beneath my feet. And the smell! The air is fresh and light. I inhale again and my body draws in a hundred scents from nature; my heart rises. I must steady myself. I watch. I move. Someone leaves the temple. I am too much in the open and might be seen. If someone carries a light, I will certainly be seen. My moves have to be better timed. Better intuited. I should stay close to the trees as long as it's possible. Too much adrenaline. My heart pounds.

I make my way again. Pushing towards the house up ahead, drawn by its lights, all the while mindful to keep my body in the dark. There will be people there, for sure. But there will also be food. I press on. Pausing. Breathing. Shifting in silence. Placing each foot with care. I pass the temple. The wind moves the trees. I hold still. Afraid. The wind falls now. I move again. Breathe again. Step. Stop. Breathe again. Then finally, the living quarters of the temple. The perfect version of my ramshackle dwelling. A gentle rustling inside as people go about their business with a pattering of feet over tatami and floors of wood; their voices soft and light, if somewhat distant.

I look in through a window now and spy a large cooking pot. Wonderful vegetables bubbling away. Steam rising. The smell, so subtle and so, so good. And I sense the heat. I must time this carefully. No one must see me. No one must hear me. No one must suspect.

But then without a second thought the moment had chosen itself, and I snuck into the kitchen and gorged myself, shovelling whatever was to hand into my mouth, almost burning myself at times. I ladled a helping of leftover miso soup, and drank it back in desperation. I forced down all kinds of vegetables as fast as I could and filled myself up with leftover noodles and pickles, grabbing also at sweet stuff, all kinds of delights, surely leftovers from the temple's many ceremonies, and all the while my temperature rising, my head growing light. I had imagined moving in swiftly and taking what I could find, perhaps not too much, return-ing to my dwelling, resting there and eating like a civilised man. It was not like that. I moved without thought, my senses on high alert, monitoring the moves of those I had seen inside the place, and those I had merely heard. If anyone surprised me I could not vouch for what I would do, the hunger filled me with a violence, a torment never known, and knives lay near at hand. As I crammed the food into my mouth I tried keenly to separate and number the voices there and held each of them distinct inside my mind, measuring their distance, willing them, ordering them, not to come near.

I fed like an animal, and like the most efficient thief I stole whatever foods lay easily in reach, filled my pockets to the brim, and I glided from that place like the expert ninja I had become.

On the way back I vomited. The shock of good food was

too much for my stomach. And eating like a hungry dog? That's not good. It can never be good. I cleaned myself up. Then I drank water, but only in small amounts. I emptied my pockets and placed the modest haul of temple food out of Cat's reach, for he clearly had his own supply. By now it was almost pitch dark, clouds wrapping the moon in a heavy woven cloth. I would rest. Then I would take the remaining food more slowly.

The last of the food still made my stomach bad. This time my bowels could not take it. I bathed and bathed, and had to bear the sensation of cramps, and the pain of the cold water as it ran over me. Not a good state. I did not truly know if rice was sufficient to keep a man, but I knew we never ate rice that was old, and though it bored me to eat only rice and at times it swelled my stomach, it did not make me sick. After the temple fare my guts made noises I could never have imagined and I begged them to go easy. Still there is pain. Perhaps I should not drink this water. I had better take to boiling it.

13.

I slept awhile. When I woke I was cold and something had happened to me. I touched my head. My hair was gone. Moonlight caught the soft white strands scattered where I lay; had someone slept beside me? Had another head rested here? I touched my head again, my hair, my thick black hair, was gone. I felt around my skull in disbelief. Not a strand there. I touched my face and felt around my neck and chin, nothing, not a single hair, not even the faintest trace of stubble. But I was surely dreaming – I put both of my hands to my head and ran them round and around it. My scalp, bare and smooth as a large and shiny fruit. Was this true? I am a young man with a good head of hair. Thick black hair. Hair that is sometimes admired. As a boy, my grandmother would gently run her fingers through it, and when she did so I would arch my back and purr, the perfectly contented cat. I had hair. Thick black hair. So what happened? And what about my chin? By now a considerable amount of stubble had grown and several long and somewhat spindly hairs that were heading towards a beard. They had ambition, and I had plans for them. Where had they gone? Is this a joke? Someone plays a trick? Did my former co-workers find me here? Did they spy on me, and out of mischief think it fun to shave off a whole head of hair? And what is this useless pile of frail white hairs here?

I checked myself over. From head to foot no hair at all, not on any part of my body.

I am become a fish. A baby. A very old man. I am twenty-five. It's not possible. Have I slept a whole lifetime through and woken only now as my elderly self? It's not possible. I can move every part of me, there is strength in my arms, my eyes can see. I am still twenty-five. I am still a young man. But I have lost my hair.

It's not good. It's far from that. But somehow I cannot let things get the better of me. So far I have not come across a mirror here, and for that I am grateful. Emaciated, hairless, my skin turned grey. For sure, I cannot venture outside, certainly not in daylight, certainly not on the street side with all its passers-by. People might have noticed me before, unkempt, a man without shoes. A stranger here. Nothing more. But now my appearance would terrify them. And how better to raise suspicion? They would summon someone, someone in authority, someone with power, officials, perhaps specialists, medics, police. They would take hold of me, question, examine and detain me. Still I would not have answers they would care for. Still I would struggle to persuade them that I meant no harm here, or even that I am who I say I am. And in this state it would be impossible to find man or woman who would vouch for me. I doubt my own family would know this wretched guy. Who would recognise me anymore? I could fail to know myself. And I would surely stand accused, or diagnosed, and either way I would be cast aside and removed somewhere, to a place of total isolation, a place without light, without windows, and no legal exit. I see it all now, and vividly. It would not go well. Whatever else, and no matter how swift my progress with the notes in here, I will now have to stay at least until my hair grows back. *How long will that be?* I cannot say. But I hope and pray it comes back soon, and thick and black, just as it was… I sweep up these limp white strands, hard to believe that these were ever mine. *What comes next? Truly. What else will come?* I don't have answers. It is as it is. But the questions had better stop. They drive a man insane. And self-pity? It only ever undermines a man.

Nothing in my head. Nothing on my head. It won't always be that way. I will have to wait. Just wait. Let things be awhile, and I will surely be restored.

I will make do with the rice a bit longer. And so what? It will last some months yet, and if I don't overly exert myself it will go further. For certain I will have recovered and left this place long before it's all used up. As for dreaming, the lack of clarity at moments; the slight, unsteady grip of reality, perhaps it is not the meagre diet that causes these symptoms, but just my state of mind, some strange internal cause, and like a machine, in some automatic way, I am generating stress, hallucinating some phantom condition. My mind, cranking things up in just the wrong way, making the body sick, perhaps for lack of stimulus? If this is this case I had better keep myself busy for longer, my mind distracted that it cannot fret or idle too long and conjure things which are not there and so insidiously steal my health.

By now I have made attempts to fix what I can in the room I sleep in despite a growing fever, but with my head now bald, perspiration simply pours over it and soon I grow cold and afterwards I shiver. I have found some cloth to cover my head and hope it will be enough. But I have to work! Longer. Harder. There is still the entire upper floor left to explore, and so many things to be noted down, yet to be made use of. The boxes. So many boxes. Perhaps a project of their own. A box dwelling? A rather brilliant box dwelling. Why not?

Tears come, but I can make no sense of them. Unless they come to celebrate the things that lie ahead? Might be. The simple anticipation of recovery bathed just now in sweet and salty tears. I let them settle on my cheeks.

Cat has arrived. He settles himself near to me. I stroke his back, under his chin, behind his ears. I have lost my hair, Cat. He does not seem to mind. He does not seem to notice. I am glad. *Soon,* I tell him, soon I will make strides again, back into the world. More behind the ears, he bids.

14.

No voices or sounds in my head these last days, and I have not sensed the presence of the shapeshifter for some time and so my courage grows. I had been determined to start on the box room but the fevered nights had left my body weak. I drastically needed to refuel but I had been retching for several days and it had been difficult to take the rice. Hard to know if I should force some down, even taking it in the smallest amounts, but my bowels were in poor shape again and I feared being in a state I lacked the strength to cope with. I could not bear it if I wasn't able to keep myself clean. I had to keep my dignity; it might be the case that this is all that can remain. And so just now I did not eat. *Eat? Don't Eat? Work? Rest? Work harder, faster, more?* It tires me. Circles. And endless contradiction. What best to do?

I lay myself back down. Days elapsed, though in truth I could not measure how many. The fever came back, then would seem to subside only to rise again. A tormenting tide. Pains shot through my head. I slept but did not feel rested. At times I dreamt. Horrible scenes. My stomach growled, perhaps for food, perhaps in anger. I could not tell. My eyes felt sore; my mouth was dry, the skin, cracked. I was hot, and cold, and my body ached throughout. At times of waking I was restless but lacked the strength to move. A man should eat. And a man should take water. This is always the minimum. But still I did not move.

Somehow, finally, I slept more decently, and in the days that followed the shapes that moved around me in the half-light, did not seem to trouble me. Perhaps the fantasy that someone watched over me. Cared, fed, and covered me. I know that I drank water. I recall it leaking from a cup, run from my lips. Someone was here then. Someone took a cloth and wiped my chin. Did I imagine that? I cannot say. But there is a cover over me just now, and I am sure that I took water.

Cat returned. Once more he swaggered in with pride, a gift between his teeth. It twitched, and with the quickest snatch of teeth, this stolen breath was to be the creature's last. I felt myself recoil. It was nature, but I wished he would not do that.

I bathed, and finally I managed some rice. Then I took a cloth and carefully I wiped away the dust from Cello. Cat removed the remains of his small prey, and returned again with eyes bright, tail high. He nestled close by. Some momentary order was restored.

After some time, and with some trepidation, I ventured into the box room. I quickly made new discoveries and easily felt lifted by this: several deep wooden boxes containing tools; inks in special glass bottles; and a few ceramic pieces – perhaps the possessions of some former artisan, for like everything else I came across they had the appearance of things abandoned long before. Covered in dust and cob-webs, I found them romantic. They seemed to ask that they be used with care and with respect and I nodded assent. I made myself some space and knelt down to examine the things more closely. After a while Cat joined me, curling his body around my back, then standing to speak in my ear.

More rummaging produced a set of make-up boxes. At first I could not identify them, just guessing at their use. Perhaps antiques. Some of them were decorated, a few were empty but many still held remnants of powders and colour. Most of them coated in dust, matted threads and hair. Some of the boxes would clean up well but for others I was not so confident. The lucky ones had been wrapped in neat cloth bags. Inside another cloth I found brushes, I guessed for the powders. The things that Yumi had were very different from these fine things. I didn't know if it mattered whether I used them for the ink, but if I found no others, then that's what I would do. Cat postured now, demanding attention, striking poses. I might try to sketch him, I thought, but later. I gave him a look and he let me alone.

At the bottom of one of the deeper wooden boxes I found combs and other old and ornate-looking hair accessories. My mother would have loved them. I ran my fingers across my bare head.

As for the stacks of cardboard boxes, these had all been rather expertly collapsed out of shape, and judging by the markings on some, were mostly packaging for household electrical goods, some of them were huge. I chose one and brought it out and into my room. My default space – I had the run of an entire house, a huge house, I could divide my needs between them, but I did not. In truth I sense that might only have added to the loneliness.

The box I picked was one of the larger ones, formerly the

cardboard casing of a refrigerator. So far I have only reassembled it in as much as it is now once again a three-dimensional, fully recognisable box shape. Even this minor move has filled me with excitement, it feels so good to return to my plans. I have also found some tape and knives which will be helpful when I come to do more intricate work on the place. Place? Why do I call it that? It is a box. Just a box. But place it is. There is no one is here. I shall do as I please. Name things as I want. A box is a house is a place.

Strange to think that I first did something quite like this under my office desk when I was still a full member of society. That box was smaller, and soon I will have constructed a superior box home. A bigger one at least. And so as to continue the theme of this current dwelling of walls within walls and holes within holes, I have decided to carve out windows and let in the light. It is also fitting that the material for my new compact dwelling will be cardboard, for I'm heavily drawn to the qualities that paper has to offer. When compressed into these clever box walls, it is, from my experience, both thoroughly sturdy and more than adequately insulating. Reasonably durable in the short term, though careful use must surely increase longevity. And I realise now, that in my box-dwelling history, I have really been most fortunate – I have so far not had to face being outdoors in a box, and have therefore not had to deal with any officials, police or general passers-by, nor have I met with drunks or anyone given to violent attacks or unkind remarks; and I have not had to consider the weather at all. Incredible good fortune. To be genuinely homeless? I try to imagine it. To be utterly without shelter and with precious little to protect you from those who would harm you, beat you, burn you; or lashing rains, the force of a storm, or in other circumstances, a penetrating heat; or deep snows and the fear of perishing in the coldest temperatures. Really. Imagine. Truly. Imagine.

Sometimes thoughts like that almost choke the life from me. I feel my head as though it is pulled from my spine. I jerk upwards in a vain attempt to breathe, to snatch a breath, to taste some life again. And I see myself in the distance, tiny, *so tiny*, and I am picked up and dropped into a similar circumstance as this, but lack the shelter of a house. A box in a street. A man in a box in a street. And rain. Cold, cold rain. I hold my breath. My lips are dry. My mouth dark and wide, *so wide*. I try again to breathe.

I kneel and reach forward and gently rest my head upon the ground. When I next encounter anyone who has fallen on such hardship I will lie prostrate at their feet.

Boxes.

There is a knife in my hand. I had better be careful for I realise that I must have been wielding it about quite absently and have created cuts in this box which I did not intend – albeit only minor penetrations, but that's no use. Not what I want. Not how to work. I take some water, letting it rest upon my tongue. I must make the best box dwelling I can. That being the intention, I will apply my best efforts just as a child would, just as a professional, just as an artist would. For I need to fill a hole inside a heart behind a wall inside another.

I must consider where to position the box, and how best to make my interventions, how best to cut the windows that the box forms a relationship with the external land-scape, the habitat here, as it presently exists. There are precise measurements at play; a sense of balance, and the box dwelling must somehow emerge in a way that is entirely in keeping with this. Principles must be applied, and in all aspects of the work I must be skilful. If further cuts are wrongly made there will be no going back. I feel rather like a surgeon. Though I know full well that I am not and no one would die here were my hand to slip. I could simply start afresh with a new box. But I will not. I desire above all else not to be wasteful, not to be frivolous – except in thought, and that, only in the pursuit of creative and, so to say, useful design. If I need to practise I will do so on 'dead' box material: the type of cardboard which, try as you might, would never make a living, breathing box dwelling. And so, I set to work on prototypes. Prototypes! That's it! And like a surgeon in training I will become skilful and assured before I attempt the work itself.

This might take some time, but cut away from the world like this, indeed, cut *out* of the world, I have something very much greater than time. I have the absence of it. The absence of time and the presence of a box. A brand new box. It's going to be wonderful.

15.

Cello watches over me as I work, and I find it ridiculous that I cannot play – if I did it would quickly be the end of things. I would be discovered here in the shadows, sitting naked like a fool – for I have long since taken mostly to being undressed. I don't have many useful clothes and feel

I should try to keep the few I have in good condition for the time that I might need them – and so, if someone came, they would find this small thin naked man without shoes or hair, in a state not easily measured or understood; a cello singing wistfully into his heart; cicadas outside crazed with love; a sack of old rice for sustenance; notes and a journal, and boxes. Boxes, sir. These are boxes. And what could they think? Useless to explain. Something bad would surely follow. And so, Cello, you will have to sing alone for now, in my heart, and in my head.

As for the box dwelling itself, rather brilliantly, it has already set new challenges. And I have started to experiment, adding in markings of my own, treating the printed refrigerator branding and associated text (dimensions, weight, model number and so forth), as the starting point from which I build up seemingly random text, something coded – and as it develops this will vary in size and hopefully offer a more interesting finish; it is also a means of embedding notes that I prefer to be kept secret (again, in the first instance I am using the dead box material to practise on). From a distance I think the box might eventually appear to have a textured finish, something not easily discerned but rather intriguing nonetheless.

And now, what is this curious sequence? It's strange how easily patterns can emerge even when trying to avoid them. I don't really want patterns because they are a reminder of the existence of time. I would rather not reference time at all. And since thoughts regarding my hair loss alternately thrust me back to babyhood – an entirely useless state just now – or forwards into old age – which would be truly unfair since I would not like to forgo the intervening years – I have decided to do more than simply ignore time, and have elected to banish it. And strangely, it might not be that difficult. I will take the move from night to day and round again as nothing more than a variation in the colour of the sky and depth of vision, and refuse to note the frequency with which this happens. Something messes with my health and attempts to steal my strength, but I will not be beaten. I return to my box.

16.

It does not work. I busy myself, body and soul inside this place, but just now my heart begins to sink. Between the stretches of work on the box and my notebooks I still pursue repair work to the house, and it is useless. My skills are limited, and some of my methods even prove self-defeating, the repairs come undone almost as soon as I have made them. This place, it creaks and shifts about, new fractures appear so easily and I struggle to patch them before they are tested once more. Sores open up everywhere, *blisters, sores, lesions.* The house, how it moans, and my attempts to soothe it are always so inadequate. The earth of late, it trembles, and again and again it jangles my nerves. On top of this, it is certain that the typhoons will gather themselves and strike again quite soon. I am choked with worry. I feel it, I feel it intensely. The enemy army of endless '*WHAT IF?s*' circle in on me. And who knows how long it takes them to deliberate, to ready and brace themselves and order their number into the most menacing interrogators, the most brutalising guards, the most efficient killing squad. At times I am certain I hear marching, I feel their tread as it shakes the ground, I picture the butts of their rifles and recoil in pain as though already knocked down by them. I touch my head; I feel the moisture there, certain it is blood.

It is sweat. It is only sweat. Now breathe. But for certain, at some point, they *will* come. And they will order an investigation, a terrifying, ruthless, sleep-deprived interrogation.

Sounds enter just now. I do not know them. Sometimes voices. Perhaps it would help if I kept notes of this. If I tried to map it. And if I took such notes, what should I do with them? They could end up as evidence and work against me. Best I don't write that stuff down. Not in any form. *Oh, but what should I do? I don't know what is real? What is sure? What is phantom? What happens? I should do something to recover myself. But what could that be?* I would lie here as still as the dead, and for days, if I thought that that would help. Would it? But I must move. That must be the better plan… *And I must eat!*

I have money … for sure I do, and so I will dress, cover my head, and bind my feet well enough that in darkness no one need care, and when the light fades I will sneak out of this place, taking the street side, and I will enter the best restaurant my nose can find and eat my fill. No one will bother overmuch. I will mind my own business, they can keep their eyes on theirs.

Still too early, too light. And truly I would shoot the sun just now if the night would come here faster. I sweat so much I begin to fear that when I step outside passers-by will think I carry some infection. I should wait before I dress, and let my body cool as night draws in. For now, I remain bare, laying out the clothes in readiness. Fresh cloth for my head, and strips to wrap my feet.

Reacquainting myself with Cello would be the perfect activity to fill this space, but since I must not play I settle myself opposite her, communicating in nothing more than the ripples on the summer heat, the tender silence hereabout.

Settled facing her, I position myself appropriately as if to play an imaginary cello, all the while enjoying the spectacle of a real and very beautiful one, as though in a mirror. I take up my imaginary bow and play. My invisible cello singing here, warm and whole in the fragrant quiet. A shiver down my too-hot spine. I grow animated and will play with great vigour. I laugh inside, and close my eyes, returned just now to childhood, to stolen time, to secret places.

Sitting alone, a man plays an imaginary cello in the hopes of winning the heart and approval of a real one. She listens attentively and applauds. A silent rapture.

It is dark outside. I have slept. But how was it that I played so hard and collapsed again into sleep? And what did I do? My legs, wrapped around my cello, the *real and true cello…* My body twisted in embrace as though she was my love. I don't know how this came about, how I come to be positioned like this. I had been sitting some distance away. I moved … I must have moved. Taken hold of her, held her close, and in my sleep my limbs grown so entirely stiff about her shape that now I cannot easily let go. In fact, I cannot feel my legs at all. Entangled, I try to move but I am in pain. How was it possible to sleep this way? And now my concern is very much greater than these few minor ailments, for since I don't know how I came to be entwined like this, what else might I have done? Swept up in emotion, and in the moment, in a kind of heat-induced, sleep-induced craze, did I forget myself, and the rule I set? That I must not truly play! Have I been playing?

The door is still closed tight. I see no signs that anyone has been inside, and if they had I would surely have been taken from here immediately. Arrested. And if the police did not come, then perhaps some casual passer-by. In that case there would be a natural delay in my arrest while they withdrew to inform the authorities of my trespass. If so, they must have done so by now, and the police are on their way, about to smash inside this place at any moment. Oh please god that this is not the case, and no officials come. If I have been witnessed in this state, lying here, my body naked, draped about a cello as though it were my lover, for certain I will end my days in a mad house, an institution aimed at the reform of such delinquent behaviour, but perhaps never fully reformed and therefore detained indefinitely. I have read of those cases. It never goes well. The people who slip through the cracks, those who withdraw or fall away from society, so entirely dispossessed not even a child would vouch for them... You have to be known, identifiable, someone must always be available to speak for you, to state your case or you really are quite lost. That being the case I had better quit this place immediately, forget everything.

Just run and run.

The door won't open. That isn't true. It will, it will. But I cannot move. It is not for the deadness, neither the cramp. In fact, I don't know what it is prevents me, but the fact remains, I cannot move. Again that isn't true. I can by now move any part of me, my limbs are painful and somewhat stiff, but in essence, everything required for moving through a doorway is operational. Then what detains me? I cannot hear anything, I see no one. What is there to frighten me?

It is dark for sure, but that is the safest condition in which to flee, to run as fast as my feet will take me from a place where I might soon be set upon. I must go before police arrive, and truly, who knows what they might do. They might be accompanied by medical specialists who will assist in my suppression, take pleasure in my sedation, collude in my detention. *I can see it!* I have to go, and now. But I simply cannot 'exit'. I hold the door; I feel the air outside. It grows quite cool just now. I must do something soon or someone will see. They might not care. But when they find themselves questioned later, and under pressure, for sure they will remember the strange little man who fled this place in haste. And still I cannot do it. I don't know why. I have closed the door.

I am losing myself, the walls fold away; the mind, with nothing to hold it … *what can it do?*

I must act. Perhaps in some extreme way. A violent rebalancing, so to speak. Some brutal measure.

And so…

I picture the foods I gorged at the temple dwelling. I see myself, the saliva; eyes grown large and round; lips cracked, parted, gnarled like the forced oyster shell. The growling in my head. The temple voices in the background, nearing. Adrenaline coursing through my body, and shots of pain, and the deep joy of flavours. My pockets, full.

I see how firmly madness has me in its grip. And I know now what I will do. And so, tomorrow, when it has grown freshly dark, I will make my second move across the temple garden. So much already lost, the rest … splintering, coming apart, taking flight. Soon there will be nothing, I expect.

Sorrows gather. Like birds they swoop.

17.

Tonight, as I enter the temple spaces my approach must be quite different. It was only luck that I was not caught out the first time, and now my ambition is very much greater, for I will make a move on the temple itself. My mind set firmly on the offertory box. From here on, what is there to lose?

A blue-black sky. I dress, and as I do so, calmly, in my mind, I carve out a course that cuts smoothly through the temple garden. I must be quick and clear in my moves. Ever more, I care to answer to no one. I place Cello in a cupboard, and close the door upon her. Not an easy thing to do. Cat looked on disdainfully, but it seemed it would be for the best.

Ready now, I place the cloth about my still-smooth head. I step outside and the darkness closes in.

It is a strange activity to wait here in the shadows, listening with such great care, trying to judge whether footsteps truly retreat or whether a lapse in tread indicates a turn on a heel and the possibility of someone's return. Some people hereabouts possess the lightest tread. I have observed one monk who quite literally seems to glide. And if I am caught by anyone it will most surely be by him, the light-footed menace.

My senses on high alert, I choose my moment. I watch for Light-foot. He is almost a shadow there deep inside the temple. I see him. His profile. He changes direction. I see his back. The edge of his robe. But then I fail to make out his movements and so I pause again. I must not step inside until I am certain of his whereabouts.

The insects make a lullaby, not much longer and their favourite season will be gone.

Lightfoot seems truly to have retreated, perhaps the end to his duties here this night. But I wait a short while longer. When I was a child we would visit the temple near our home, and I remember the fun of dropping the coins my mother gave me deep into the offertory box. I liked the sound of them as they shivered against the wood and crashed against the coins there down below, invisible save for a tiny glimmer in the deep dark box – and perhaps I only imagine the last part, still, I take it as memory.

My hands sweat. I hang my head in shame, but I see no other way. You are the man you have come to be. I did not want to be a thief but so it is. I face what I have become. Back at my dwelling the silk tie slipped from the lacquer box so easily, and the money inside climbed into my hands. I glance back across the garden. The wind is getting up. A tree shakes itself in front of the moon as though it dances for favours. I almost fell, losing my footing in the darkness; someone's voice? Light-foot? But no one comes. The air is still again. I step and breathe alternately. I drop my paper money, the gambling stash in its entirety, between the wooden slats, careful that it is not taken by the wind. But why the tears? My chest is tight, but full of joy. Relief.

Back at my place once more I take off my clothes. Small, tight, dirty muscles on bones too thin. I gaze around in the darkness. Still besieged by hunger. My fat and greedy eyes that would devour all. Wild as a dog. A man can last some while without food. This I have come to know. Rice and water, it's enough. It must be. But for all my father instructed me upon, there is something that he missed:

Whatever else in life, *don't ever, be a shit!*

AUTUMN

1.

A man with no more substance than a pencil drawing, an image scratched in sand.

I checked the surface of my hands. I no longer knew them to be mine. My toes had begun to move at times in an involuntary way, as though they might leave without the rest of me. No one would choose to be depleted like this, but in some last urgent moments, you have to take hold of things and, at your weakest point, somehow find strength.

I needed to take stock. I realised that my plan to escape time was hugely flawed. Such a fool! Wanting to live outside or beyond it? It really isn't possible, because the idea, the reflection, at the very least, an impression will remain no matter what. And being detached or disconnected? That's not so simple either. I had truly thought I might banish time, or hoped at least to ignore it well enough. I imagined I could throw it off, just as I might a jacket, that I could lay it down somewhere, and that it would lie there inert, that it would not trouble me. That's not how it is. It seeks you out. And even without the devices that count away our lives in the smallest increments, you cannot readily escape the moon as it rolls away the sun, and you cannot ignore the dance and battle of nature as it wrestles leaves from trees or forces blossom from tight-fisted buds.

Here, the temple chrysanthemums have withered and the distant maples reveal a change in season whether I want to admit it or not. And though I cannot deny the beauty of those crisp red leaves against a bright and brutal sky, they are evidence of my many long weeks here. Autumn has come. There is much to do.

Without another thought I threw myself into my work as though operating on reserve tanks, driven by a kind of self-annoyance, impatience, the need to push on, to make things happen, to get things done, and what I had in mind now for the boxes was really far from the improvised dwelling of my office days. Ideas streamed through my head. A viral highway, an ice-cold sake feeling, and with it, the sharp rush of adrenaline I got from placing bets – truly, not a bad feeling at all.

At first I took an experimental approach, tearing at the cardboard, savaging the boxes I deemed spare and sacrificial, fashioning them however I wanted, however I could, with whatever my fractured mind and calloused hands would permit. I pushed myself, doing whatever it took to get me to the prototypes. Then I practised how to carve into the boxes, carefully, and with little damage to the walls. Rows of dead boxes mounted up neatly about the room, whilst others lay strewn across the floor, proof of my frustration and lack of skill. Getting the lines exact and leaving the corners intact (those I wished left intact) was troublesome, but I did it.

Next up was the coding. I had decided long before that I would not write the code in any known language but invent my own. A code within a code, so to speak, that no one, unless making a deliberate investigation of it, would recognise it as a means of communication at all. And indeed, perhaps it is not, if it communicates with no one but myself. Is that what I intend? There's no way to answer. But I have worked at this in the manner of a complete fanatic. One of the trickiest parts has arisen over the use of ink, and trying to prevent it from bleeding into areas I would rather it did not. And yet some of these accidents have led to intriguing designs. Perhaps they are, rather, anti-designs, since they were not intended. And so, excited by this, I have named them:

'The anti-designs of Takeo Tanaka'
- created by an ordinary guy, with ordinary eyes -

I pause for water. There are deep cuts now to one of my hands, but mostly on my fingers. I didn't notice, I didn't feel anything, but I had better wrap them. The green strip from the insect box is dirty. I had better root around for something else. Truly, not even a rat lives like this. Ha!

Alright then, the upper floor. Let's see what lies up there. I breathe. Strange to think I have not climbed these steps before. The journey up is brief; and since they are old and wooden, the stairs creak just as I imagined. An oddly reassuring sound, and I step lightly as though concerned I might disturb someone.

The sun lies in a broad stretch up here, and slants its weight heavily through the windows, thick and yellow. It seems it takes up residence and is not merely passing through. It is musty up here, and the dust lies heavy. I stand awhile, the light upon my back, for I have been too long away from sunlight and its warmth upon my skin. After some moments scanning the room my eyes settle on a series of long slim drawers, wooden with neat handles. Row upon row. Something magnificent. I wonder what they hold. Perhaps special drawings, or maps, but certainly some great treasure, for no one made cupboards like this for ordinary things. They slide open with ease. A mark of precision. But no map. And no rare manuscript. I take each drawer now with extra care, for I must not bleed on them. Teasing them open from the outer edges with the one hand and, using my face and chin, I evolve somehow a funny but effective way to take the drawer a little further. There is cloth of some sort, fine cloth. Silk. Folded neatly. I take it out. A very fine kimono. In the other drawers the same. On closer inspection they are the finest I have seen. But what are they doing here? No one comes to this place. No one uses them. It seems that no one misses them? I have not quite opened all the drawers but as far as I see they each hold a woman's gown, and it is curious, but this discovery has lifted my spirit greatly. Gently, I slide them back again each inside its wooden bed. How sad that they just lie there. For now I let them alone, resting in their own clever space. But for sure I will visit them again.

A thin trail of blood marks my journey. Nothing here to bind my hand. I had better wash the green silk strip, it might do well enough.

2.

Once the silk had dried I kept the fingers of my left hand bound up tightly. Then I stole upstairs again and took out one of the kimonos, it had to be acceptable to use just one. I took it as a coat, draped about my shoulders. Truly, what a wonderful thing. I thought about the elegant and fashionable kimonos I had seen at different times in my life, and also the simple ones, the rather basic, practical ... *versions* ... 'types'... my mind driven suddenly now, and high speed, back to the prototypes. *This was what it was all about!* First, there is always a prototype, a basic type, always, of anything, and from there you adapt, you develop. Adding, subtracting, fine-tuning. There was no way to guess if there would be a demand for beautiful dwellings in miniature, perhaps not, but I knew there was need of box dwellings. A great need.

When a person faces challenging times they do not lose their desire for comfort. And beautiful or not, they need shelter. In my case, I have lived in a box inside a building, so to say: a box inside a box, but there is huge scope to adapt this box home. Huge! And perhaps I could specialise, focussing my attention entirely on the plight of those who find themselves homeless, improving the box dwellings, rendering them capable of surviving the perils of street life, of rural outdoor life, of post-disaster landscapes... Boxes. That's all that we need. My spirit lifts.

Filled with eagerness and mischief, I hunted around the place some more. What else might I make use of? What more is there in here that will inspire? It was a pure and private pleasure to discover each new room alone like this. And insane that I had not done so already somehow. But anyway, who cares! House, I am getting to know you!

Straw and bamboo hats sit in an adjoining room, another brilliant find, a huge stack of them. I like their shape, their texture, and how they are constructed. And I am deeply curious about the materials: straw and bamboo – cheap and natural, adaptable... I might find other uses for them and they will surely last quite well. Typically, I know they have been worn by farmers and other outdoor workers for hundreds of years, and this has to bode well. They use them even now. Such a simple sort of headgear, keeping off the sun, protecting from the rain. Cleverly woven. It must be the weave that provides the strength, or does that merely increase it, enhances it perhaps? The weave accounts for their flexibility also? For sure they are robust. I like these questions. I like this simplicity. I like it a lot. Oh, I wish that Cat was here; we might dance awhile to celebrate. Impressive longevity, that might be the most important quality they have to offer; and varied application, especially bamboo. I will teach myself to weave, and see what other discoveries can be made. As for the boxes and the prototypes, I have decided for a time to work some of these in shoji paper. I need to further conserve the box supplies, so I will store them out of the way, there are a few plastic sheets that I can use to cover them; and I thought to cut and carve bamboo struts to reinforce the shoji boxes.

Dismantling some hats just now, unweaving to weave, I make notes as I go and sketch a few ideas. I am curious as to how they are constructed. Then I weave some afresh and others into something new, nothing too ambitious, mere shapes, whatever they will take, small practice elements. I collect up junk and reconfigure it, shaping, making, re-making, making better, and discarding that which does not work so well. Truly, there is an entire world inside this place. If the world rejects a man, he must simply make his own.

3.

I have slept some good long while and deeply. I touch my head. Still entirely smooth. The skin on my body, rough to the touch, thin like paper. The light filters in as though it dresses me. A yellow wash over dust and dirt-covered limbs. Black and purple bruising. I reach for the kimono but it is gone. I look about, but can't see it. And now that I am fully awake I feel certain that though I have slept (I think perhaps waking and sleeping on again), something here has been coming and going, almost as though there was a flow somehow in keeping with the rhythms of my sleep. Something comes here, I know it – *the shapeshifter?* – and it has been coming here perhaps some while now, and yet I do not see it. Why not? I don't know if it truly stays when I am sleeping, but afterwards there is the trace of something, and an impression I have of a presence and of repetition. Then there is the time that I sipped water from a vessel, did I dream that? But wasn't a cover then placed over me? That seems gone … I can't recall. Does it mess with me? This thing? Really, I am a fool, I ought to be mindful, for though it has not so far harmed me, that might not always be the case. I have shown so little concern, and I know full well what happens when I am too casual in my behaviour. I cannot deny that I am an intruder here myself, perhaps small proof that not all are dangerous or pose a threat – but still, it would be wise to take more care. But truly, I don't understand why I have not yet seen it.

I look around again for the kimono. It's not here. Perhaps I didn't wear it? I dreamt that too? I bolt upstairs. There it hangs! Placed as though with care, as my mother or aunt might do, that it might air well enough. The lining is dirtied, proof of my clumsy use. But I did not bring it up here. I took it, that's for sure, but I did not take care of it, and I would not think to air it. Well, there are sounds now, and I'm not certain if they are inside or outside my head. Steadily, I take the steps back down to my room again. Somewhat faint, I sit cross-legged, and close my eyes awhile.

Right in this moment I am certain I hear the creature now as it enters this place, my senses on high alert. The shapeshifter, it comes. Making its entrance through a narrow window in the kitchen. I am sure of it. I keep myself still, tilting my head to gauge the sounds, not daring to move further for fear of alerting it to my whereabouts. The lightest, swiftest movements, the faintest sounds. Then a shuffling as though it makes itself comfortable. I cannot be sure, but my suspicion is that it is taking up a position on a long slender shelf through there. I have never been so sharply aware of it, the air still. My skin shivers. I need to unfold my legs, grown stiff, and I do this with the utmost care. My thoughts and perceptions might still be unreliable, and sounds bend about a place, but this is the best sense I can make of what I hear. I listen now for more.

I must have laid my head down. But I cannot remember. What happened? It seems I lost consciousness. Did someone hurt me? I check myself over. Or was it only sleep? I look about. Was I made to drink something? There is the residue of something, I know not what, lying on my tongue. I wipe my finger over it. It is dark in colour, slightly thick. Medicine? Poison? Was something done to me? I don't hear anything now. The shapeshifter? Where has it gone? I listen. Nothing. All around it is dark, and what amount of time has passed? Just the day? More? There is no vessel nearby, but I drank something. Didn't I? Certainly something bitter passed my lips. My skin is wet as though I have some fever. Did someone tend to me?

I search around again, my eyes pushing at the dark. I breathe. I try to recall the night. I remember my body. Hot and clammy. I remember sweat. Some liquid in my throat. I swallowed. I believe I have been sleeping for short snaps of time... I would wake, and each time I did so I was made to wonder just what I had been doing. Sometimes it was clear, boxes around me, my journal laid open, and I would surface in some awkward position, hat or pen in hand. Bamboo splints. But at other times I made no sense of my surroundings. No thoughts at all, and then too many. *And were they even mine?* I realise now, like mad rabbits, they would hop in, and spring out, or take up residence, choking the space up in my head, and never but never could I find what I was looking for. Never the right box. Always at the back. Dust covered. My mind – a warehouse. Inside are boxes. None of them mine.

In the darkness now I lie on my back, arms behind my head for comfort, legs crossed. I stare at the walls. I consider the cruel way in which I have looked upon vagrants and migrants, those I took for criminals, or low-born pigs. I regarded them as though their very existence made me sick. I see that. I see the distance. The past. A stretch of time and space. And I? I, am sick. *And so what?* By now I despise even my own thoughts, and the part of me that wants to return to what I had before. I do not want to be as low as I am now ever again in my life. I want to be safe and comfortable, above the sewage of society, not even thinking of them in case it weakens and infects me and renders me the same.

Not even looking down on the desperate, and the dispossessed, just not thinking of them at all!

Box up the inferior. Close the lid. Push the box aside.

I am a pencil-drawn man.

4.

If I had a fever, it has gone now. Still the faint residue of something on my tongue. I have taken water but somehow it remains. An unpleasant, viscous residue.

I enter the kitchen, not sure what I might find, but there is nothing I can take as proof of intrusion, and no great clue as to the shape the creature takes, its presence still benign. No sign of Cat. I cook some rice, but only a very small measure, for the grains will soon run out.

More than anything just now I wished I might feed upon this season's fresh new rice. The last of this sack tastes all the poorer now that I witness the change in season, and know full well that far away back home the new rice would just have been harvested. Surely already celebrated and gorged upon. But it would sap my strength to grow too sentimental. Better switch the thought.

Later, I laboured at the coding hardly making a sound so that I might listen out quite well. It occurred to me that this awakening of curiosity for the shapeshifter might signal a stage in my recovery. In the last hours I had certainly felt my senses more reliable. The speedy progress I was making with the coding also seemed a good measure of this improved state. Credible thoughts zipping along now nicely. And when the mind is in good order surely everything else will follow. I speculated that it might not be more than a matter of days before I began to see signs of a fuller transition, back to myself. I checked my head and body for hair, nothing yet, but for sure this would come back soon now. Truly, what a thought! And more than that, perhaps I would not simply be returned to myself, but emerge rather as an improved version, almost as though I had been myself in training all along, and so, in all regards, a prototype of self!

I had to do whatever I could to aid this recovery, to capitalise on the energy. It might be the case that timing was crucial. I sat again, cross-legged, torso straight, I pictured myself, a soldier perhaps lost in a forest, the lone survivor of his kind, sensing the importance of maintaining strength and stamina. Of building, and rebuilding.

Now was the time to push myself. To forge ahead, to push and push. Following this simple meditation, I then ran on the spot like a fiend, completed exercises with intense vigour, endless, endless press-ups. A headstand. The best I could, the very best I could manage. What happened to me? A quiet revolution? A violent riot? My mind raced about and I wondered what else might come! My heart pounded. I breathed and took some water.

I settled myself in the alcove. Resting my feet high up on the wall. I thought of Cello.

Sounds of movement in the kitchen.

I rolled down quickly, crept close by and spied. I could not breathe. Excited. Afraid. Something bounded across the surfaces, then leapt to the floor, nudging the rice sack as though to remind me of its state.

Cat.

I returned to my activities, calmed.

My thinking clear just now. My mind, sharp.

5.

This transitional spurt of mental and physical energy would neither last nor grow unless I found some other form of nourishment, I knew this and I needed a plan. I made the best use I could of this rush of clarity, focussing hard, but also freely. Then quickly finessing ideas, half filling a notebook, possibilities now almost running with themselves, leapfrogging one over the other, for what might I do next? What should be considered in order to rebuild the self? The box, as it had been, all flattened out, might not be reassembled quite as it was, indeed, something much better might be fashioned… why not? Thoughts spilled: *nutrition, medicine, farming; movement, mechanics, stillness* … but they settled, and centred ultimately, and rather brilliantly, on the headstand. In a sense it was far too simple, but I could see now both a fabulous and natural way by which I might both stimulate hair growth and gain sustenance. And I called this:

'The Planting'

It was going to involve a certain amount of training. The

'grand preparation' – for I needed to build the strength in my arms in order to maintain the headstand for a good amount of time, and so, every evening following a general work-out and push-ups, I would practise, steadily increasing the length of time I held position by small increments. It was tough going, but I was surprised at how much could still be achieved in a determined, albeit theoretically weakened state. The sense of blood rushing to the head is something I found perturbing, and there was nothing here that could settle me well enough afterwards, and so I just had to bear the giddiness. And stand on my head I must.

I don't know a great deal about horticulture and am not well read on the subject of medicine (better to say that I know almost nothing), but I had to try whatever I could to stimulate further advancement. And if I didn't take action now, I didn't know how long it would be before I plunged into a ditch of slippery self-pity once more, perhaps this time never to climb out. Truly, this was my chance.

Just a few more nights of practice, and under cover of darkness, I would set out into the temple garden. I had planned the very spot, so to say: a blind spot, and there I would plant my head. For if I could not be nourished from the inside, then I would draw in sustenance by some other route. I would plant my head, that the earth and all its rich nutrients feed and restore me.

As for the shapeshifter, it should know that eventually I would find it. I would find it for sure, for *I would know what it is, and what it is about*. For the time being, I had to let go. There was a plan to carry out.

6.

The night has come. I have prepared my scalp in readiness for planting, bathing it in water and patting it only gently so that the surface remains slightly damp and soft and therefore, hopefully, more yielding and receptive to the nourishment on offer.

I have dressed in dark-coloured garments, I will not easily be seen, and I will wrap my feet in cloth dyed with ink, for it might look strange once I am in position should anyone happen to pass by or look out from the temple to see two pale feet seemingly suspended in the air – one metre, fifty centimetres from the ground. It would surely draw someone's attention, and worse, it would raise the alarm. The person would fear they too had seen a shapeshifter and an investigation would begin. I would have the appearance perhaps of something in possession of supernatural powers, able to condense my being into nothing more than human feet. I might be executed on the spot. Whatever else it would result in my being found out.

The feet, they are secure and wrapped now. I breathe, but too heavily. Aware that I must bring this under control before I step outside, I kneel awhile.

It seems that I am fully prepared, at least, this is the best that I can do. I tell myself all will be well. I check my clothing one last time, the feet bound and ready, movement constricted to a degree, but I do not have to move very far and so I am sure to bear it. Sucking in the first of the air outside, I make my way. The lights on the temple side are never fully out, but I have monitored the situation for a while now and have become accustomed to the patterns and routines of life there, and I am confident that this is truly the best moment. There ought to be just enough light that I can find my way without stumbling but not sufficient light that I am seen. I must also keep my head entirely covered over until the planting itself or it will surely have the appearance of a second moon, or worse still, an airborne root vegetable. I have never heard of a shapeshifter taking on the guise of something like daikon before, and I would not appreciate being mistaken for such a thing.

I must act with caution, with precision of movement, and with the silent tread of the most accomplished ninja.

Out in the evening air I feel wired. More alive in any real sense than I have felt in so very long.

The ground is curious beneath my bound feet. I tread carefully across gravel areas and step onto moss. Leaves have fallen. I had not factored that in. I had best avoid them though I would very much like the sensation of walking on their sharp crisp crackle, a reminder of youth somehow. I feel my breath and a tightness begins to bind itself about my chest. I take my steps cautiously, my head still covered and downcast so that my eyes do not give me away or settle on any distraction. I rely on my hearing to alert me to the presence of anyone moving through the garden; generally at this time the temple people are all indoors, and it is rare that anyone comes at this hour. I must relax my breathing.

I realise there is the possibility that the shapeshifting intruder crosses my path this night, perhaps as it arrives. I have so far been sure that the creature enters each time through just the one window on the far side of the dwelling, reached by the shadowy street beyond, so it has no need of moving through the garden and risks its own exposure if it comes here. Just now it is the light-footed menace that is most likely to cause difficulties. I can only hope he doesn't vary his routine this night, and keeps himself indoors. Despite my hope to gain nourishment from the ground, I will not be stealing in any literal sense, and though I have no right to be in this place, this time I enter only the temple gardens, I will not trespass further. But Light-foot would have no way of knowing this, and I can only hope that, should I be seen, my moves are not misinterpreted. Well, I must simply not be seen!

I have arrived. My heart hammers. This is the spot. The place I had chosen from my window. It seems to be just as suitable as I thought, shielded partly by several rows of bamboo. The planting will require some feat of concentration if I am to make an elegant headstand, and that is only possible if I can do so without fear of discovery.

In the first instance I must prepare the ground. I have no tools for this. I had considered using something from the dwelling, but this seemed too cumbersome. I only need to create a hollow capable of taking in my scalp, and I can do that with my hands. They make quite the roughest tools in any case, the skin has thickened and hardened so that I do not recognise them since I have used them mainly for rough chores and craftwork. Strange to consider the difference between these calloused, hardened spades and the rather soft fingers that once committed to no greater labour than casually moving over electronic screens or tapping at a keyboard.

I dig away like a dog about to bury treasure, and the idea warms me, but it is more important than ever that I remain in control of my thoughts and energy or I will fail in this. Nothing that could be a distraction, no matter its amusement or warmth must enter my head now, in fact, I seek only to empty it, for I will fill it up afresh from the ground, and the earth will nourish me.

There, my place is ready. A small and simple bed for a small and simple head. I take one last look behind the bamboo curtain, there is nothing, and a human would easily give themselves away on such a still and tranquil night. My home, in the distance, is just as I would anticipate, entirely undisturbed; the other temple buildings reveal nothing more than distant light, and I hear only the very fringes of light chatter as it drifts there far away, but no, there is almost no activity hereabouts. Alright then, I am comfortably alone.

The shallow bed that I have dug is soft. I let a few tears fall, smooth and transparent, and watch as they disperse, drops of light almost. No sadness on my part. I am far from that. I think only to prepare the ground as best I can.

I check the ink binding on my feet and ankles, all quite secure; and then perform my preparatory stretches. My heart light; my mind focussed on the task. Just now the cloth that hides my face slipped, I caught it, recovering the situation swiftly. A minor complication, soon secured again. I keep watch, listening out with care. The very last checks are made. Conditions are in my favour, but I must keep my wits. I breathe and, taking my time, I remove the cloth at the last moment, and make an elegant headstand.

Clean movements minimising my disturbance of the world out here and drawing no attention; and, as efficiently as possible I plant my scalp in the ground that it might, for a short time, find itself tied to the earth whilst Takeo Tanaka returns for the moment to the womb, joined once more to his mother, loved and nourished there.

7.

I manage to maintain my upside-down position quite well. Making it last. But it should have occurred to me that since I lack any real knowledge of plant life, this experience was set to be something greater than curious. Attempting to plant my un-plant-like self is now the most unique event in my life. It is bizarre, and yet entirely comfortable. My head feels securely embedded and supported, but more than that, it feels surprisingly natural. I am utterly at ease. It is an upside-down bliss. So comfortable that it seems completely and utterly normal and the right thing to do. As peculiar as it might appear, I feel that I have done nothing more than follow some internal drive, my gut feeling, so to speak, my instinct, and I cannot imagine deriving such a feeling of liberation from any other activity.

I would find it impossible to construe my behaviour as anything deviant or truly offending. I am harming no one and nothing, and cause no inconvenience. So, as peculiar as it would seem to anyone I might tell, and more so to anyone who happened to pass by, I feel no need to explain or justify this action. The sensation of moisture and soil against my skin is one I would pay for. It offers an unusual comfort, a very particular soft warmth. So elated, I am almost glad for my hair loss in order to have the opportunity of this unique sensation. There would be no way to appreciate this encounter with the earth if there was hair to divide us.

In many senses I feel as though I am truly naked just now (though I am still entirely robed; my feet still tightly bound); and like a babe, perhaps as yet unborn, I am fed and cared for, nourished as though from within; swishing gently to and fro in my thoughts as though in the tender confines of the womb; or as though I am nothing more than the tall bamboo there as it bows gently to the wind. Light rainfall slips and whistles around on a sudden and mischievous wind as it cuts in from the side. It echoes strangely in my ear. The droplets of rain sound heavy as they pass my ears so closely; they land heavily like overripe fruit, and water the earth. I feel a tiny river of rain as it travels the curves of my ears and it tickles. A shiver about my neck.

It has fallen quiet again. I sense it is time enough in this position. I have been here a good and happy while, but I cannot risk being found. I must now gently return. I bring down my legs and tuck them in neatly, trying to leave as little impression as possible on the delicate night, disturbing not the air, creating no ripples that might draw attention, the least reverberation; if it were possible, leaving no trace at all. I am crouched down, and must quickly cover over my scalp, firstly to avoid being seen and secondly, in an effort to keep safe that nourishing and soil-rich caress, to maintain and preserve its restorative properties. Something rises in my heart just now and I must stifle a feeling of joy or it will surely escape from me, and I cannot vouch for this being unvoiced as I would like to jump to my feet and yell out for what I feel just now is pure elation.

I check myself over again. My head is covered, my hands are free again. I place my right hand a moment on my chest to calm it. But now what happens? The clear tread of someone nearing. Someone comes? It cannot be. Please, please, it cannot be.

I picture myself turned to stone and turn my breathing inwards that I do not disturb the air, if only that were possible. I close my eyes. I am not here. I am not here. I cannot be seen!

I do not know how I managed to remain so still so long, but finally the walker has moved away. I dared not peer out, but I know full well it is possible I was seen, naive to think otherwise, and yet ... if I was seen, why did the walker not challenge me? Why didn't they come closer, speak, even kick at the stone-like figure to see what I was about, what business I had here? I cannot work it through. And I have to get back to my house. Which I, fool man, left completely unattended. But I had better fill in this hole, cover it back over. Leave no trace. I scratch at the ground and battle this intractable sense of urgency to get home as soon as I can. I have to check the house over immediately, to make sure that no one has come there, that no one lies in wait. And what of the shapeshifter? Was it here just now? It can't have been. Surely it can't, or it risked discovery every bit as much as myself. And it lacked my specific purpose here, so for sure, for sure, it can't have been. The walker here tonight was certainly human. I know this by the tread, and I do not truly believe the intruder that enters my place is human. It's possible that the shapeshifter took human form while it ventured here, but it makes no sense, the sight of a stranger would draw attention. It would rather take some animal form, a racoon dog or a palm civet, allowing it to move about the gardens with ease. No, the walker here was not my intruder, of that I feel certain. I realise now that the most likely candidate is the light-footed menace. That stupid monk. Is it possible? Was it him? In this instance the tread was anything but light. And since I know, or at the very least, suspect, that Light-foot means me no good (sneaking around at times, arrogantly parading his good looks, as he is apt to do), he is sure to have laughed at me on the spot, or to have hounded me out, held me up for ridicule, or dragged me from this place and to the police. But who else? I cannot resolve it. I have to get back, and yet I hesitate, my courage lost.

I settle myself on the ground awhile. Light rain falls. I press down the soil here, then lift it again and attempt to sift it through my fingers. I have to take hold of this distress or it will soon give me away, and all the nourishment I have been in receipt of will count for nothing if I do not keep the body calm and allow it gently to tickle its way in and strengthen me. My mother would impress this on me in my youth: the need to take adequate time about things, and this so often with regard to eating: to sit and carefully digest so as not to upset nature's rhythms; and since this is an entirely new way for a human being to take nourishment, then I imagine it calls for even greater care and attention. I am, by now, a far more complex prototype. Or perhaps a simpler one! The planted man.

I must return home and settle myself comfortably in the quiet before anyone else sees me. It rains more heavily and I grow cold.

I almost cannot believe my eyes, but as I raised my head just now, I witnessed Light-foot in the distance. Has he seen me? I have been locked in position so long in fear, and now again I'm almost paralysed – this time in fury. As I glanced up and witnessed the quickening in his step as he moved there, right to left, back towards the temple, I was left with a strong impression that only moments before he had closed a door behind him. My door. It is a trace, a shadow of perception, but I truly sense the remnants of this activity in his movements, the motion and angle of his body as he glided past, the position and movement of his hand; the tilt of his clean-shaven head. I am sure he has not long since left that dwelling and closed that door. Is it possible? Has he trespassed in my home, my dwelling, my workshop? And there witnessed the results of my many hours of joyous private labour on the prototypes, my beautiful paper dwellings, those I am making before embarking on the ultimate box. *The ultimate box? I call it that?* It seems that way, and I should not, for the words make me tremble. It's never good to deal in extremes. *The ultimate.* That's not good. What pressure. Things need to be measured, balanced, perhaps, at times, modest. Extremes force all else to fall away, to be judged too harshly. It is a sickness. I must stop myself, sit down calmly somewhere safe, and contemplate what it is I mean by such a thing. Do I truly harbour this idea and expectation, this extreme desire? I do not know. It may be nothing more than vanity, impetuosity, I am capable of both. *But what is it … and what would it be … this ultimate box?* I shiver again. In any case, whether the internal declaration holds true or not, I must limit the thought until later.

The rain steadily increases as I wait, biding my time. I feel it wiggle its way inside my clothes and underneath the bindings. Ink runs from the scarf about my head and stings my eyes. How shall I see? Such intense stress to stand wrapped up like this in the darkness. My eyes smart again and again, and this autumn rain makes me cold. Out here, just the moon for a friend. Just a lone figure below a big dappled moon. What a sad feeling grips my heart. I bend here like old pampas grass, then I look up at my moon friend, and really wonder at what I have become. I am sad, but strangely I could laugh. Out here and with my head in the ground like that, I felt true joy. And this in a way I have never known before. And yet it seems, a joy so easily lost! It seems it might be time to make my move. I look around. No one about. I have to get to the house. The menace has not re-emerged from the temple, and there are no fresh lights switched on. I sigh as I struggle like wet grass with bound feet, back to my dwelling.

8.

Closing the door, being back inside, I feel safe again, and contemplate a return to a more balanced state of mind – the palpations in my chest coming to rest, a gentle tingle in my feet.

Forgetting myself, I leant against a wall, it groaned, bidding me to stop, straw and clay crumbling against my hand. So strange to feel such a great sense of safety in a house that might at any moment fall about my ears.

The rains gather now at a powerful rate, the downpour so heavy the water begins to find its way inside this place. I hear it slipping through in many places, and already the air is different for its effect. But there is something else. Moisture rises and with it something attractive, I would even say, seductive. I smell food, but as though the aroma begins, this time, inside this place.

Someone *has* been here. A trespasser. I should not have ventured out, should not have left the place unattended. In a fury I clench my fist. But I had already guessed as much! Suspected as much! So what is the anger? To know that my suspicions have grounds? What is it, what is it truly that I feel? Fear? I was sure that Light-foot had been in here, was certain I had seen him leave this place. I remember his movements, the position of his hands. *Has he really been inside this place?*

A bowl of noodles in the shadows. Still hot. Truly, there is plenty of heat in them. Ramen. Oh, why do I weep? And how can only half a man, such as I am, find himself in possession of a whole man's tears? I am wet and cold and should get out of these rough bindings before I sit and take this food, but I lift the bowl and the tasty aroma drives me insane! I want to impose discipline. I want above all else to be civilised. And I can. I just have to keep my pace. I put the bowl down and remove the textile layers, unwinding, unbinding as though I am a gift. What happened to my skin? Veins appear at the surface where they did not lie before. And as I undress more and more fine blue-green lines erupt as the cloth falls away, tributaries. I am a map. A blanched and inky map. I hop about just now, unwrap the last of myself, and yes, all over I am marbled. I can pose as though I am a great statue from the Western world. Like this, someone might even quite like me. Is that possible? It might be so.

Well, it seems that my endeavours to recover myself are working in some small measure, though I am clearly far less recovered in any normal sense, but rather, am transformed, transmogrified. I hail from somewhere far away with a blazing sun and an ice-blue, sky-blue sea. I am a map of some unknown place, a place of fertile soils and sparkling rivers. Yes. I am a map.

Well, Takeo, it is no good to be so distracted, you must eat, and so I do. The marbled man takes his seat, and though cold and damp, he is warm inside. He will be warmer still with this fat bowl of ramen to feed upon. The steam has faded, but the soup is tasty and the noodles soothe a too-dry palate. Bliss.

It is strange, but again, treated to a meal that is anything other than old yellowed rice, my stomach is in knots; and the flavours, savoury and distantly familiar, almost cause my head to ache. And now that I have finished, my stomach is swollen, as though I carry a child.

I ate too quickly of course. But if I can sleep now, my body can surely settle itself. Nutrition now from two sources! Lucky man that I am! Perhaps all the goodness I have been exposed to will join forces inside and make a good start on the rebuild, the remake, the reconstructed Takeo. I lie here and smile at the thought, and stroke my ample aching belly.

9.

I must not have slept long, for still the night is here and it is dark outside as I wake up. Faint slips of light lie in curious configurations on the walls. My mind feels strangely easy.

I sit up and try to make things out in the darkness. The ramen bowl has gone. It cannot have gone, and so I conclude that I must be dreaming for I know the meal of noodles to have been real for I feel its effect and know it helped me sleep. I might also factor in the nourishment I received from the earth, but I cannot think it would have left me with this heavy feeling in my abdomen. No, the noodles were real, and I can no more explain the arrival of the ramen than the removal of the bowl. I have checked around the place and in the kitchen, but I do not see it, and I cannot devote any more energy to this new puzzle for the rain I have benignly witnessed as it spluttered its way in now gushes in through an increasing number of openings, and how it swells the walls. Will they withstand this?

I cannot account for my reaction, or rather, my inaction. I have remained cross-legged, just sitting here in the darkness, and though aware that I am cold, I watch in a kind of paralysed wonderment as one window after another yields to the power of the rains. Around me water gathers. I cannot just sit and watch all this as though I am truly made of stone; and if my skin was indeed a map I am not convinced it could lead me to safety. I grow excessively cold now, and if I do not move and cover myself soon I am very likely to slither away in these rising waters like an eel enveloped by some giant tidal movement.

I am quite afraid. Is that why I don't move? *Where is the sense? A typhoon blows in!* It is the season. I pinch my arm as though to check that all of this is happening, that it is real. That I am real. I should have planned for this. It's really no good to just sit still.

So many things already sodden, walls and shoji drenched. So fast! The water rises as though the ground beneath would raise it up, I scramble up the steps to my kimono store.

For a moment I thought I saw Cat. I called after him. But he's not here or did not catch my voice. I worry for his safety, but cats might survive such situations better than many. Most likely he has found himself the safest spot. I hope so.

Shut off up here, the storm seems less intense, at least the waters cannot gather round my feet, and I do not need to sit and watch them rise – a sea inside, drinking in, gulping down my home. I should have shored the place up properly. Instead I have dabbled in design and made only the most basic attempts to fill the holes here. I vow just now to fix the place as best I can once this is over. Too late, my efforts. Insufficient all around.

Best I keep my wits and find some good distraction till this passes. The kimono put to air is gone. No way to explain this, and so, shivering, I have dressed myself in fresh robes from the special drawers here, truly, the most ridiculous finery, and all of them women's for I find no other kind. And so, another beautiful kimono now hangs on too-thin shoulders. Only hours before my stomach looked and felt as though I might indeed carry a child and now, here I am, dressed in the most elegant gown as though I might be a woman of great taste and high social standing. Already it is affecting my movements. I do not mean so much that it is restricting (though in part this is the case), but rather that I feel emboldened, mischievous, playful, and in some curious way, liberated. What a thing. I move about up here and feel I am floating, light, ethereal. I move my hands and arms trying to approximate the finer movements of a woman. I do not know what woman I have in mind. And so crazy to think I have a sense of what it is to be a woman. And what kind of woman? They vary a great deal ... it might be that women vary from one to another far more than men... Most of my former work colleagues were male, and there was not so much to distinguish between them. But every woman I have known seems to have been unique – my mother, for example, is not like my aunt, my aunt and mother were not at all like my grandmother; and Yumi is not like my work friend, Shizuka, not in any way at all.

I have never thought of this before, but, *what woman am I?* I dance about the room and sense myself blush as I attempt to imitate the mannerisms and movements of some elegant, highborn woman. I cannot be certain of the accuracy or authenticity of my moves. This is just what I imagine. I cup my hand to my cheek in some excessive and coquettish move, and place my feet upon the floor in the most delicate and precise manner. But is this really 'woman'? Nothing more than a poor and worthless caricature, for sure that is the case, but just for these moments I lose myself, I become something else, and dancing here, I imagine that I am beautiful. I am a woman. I am a shapeshifter.

The touch of the fabric about my neck causes the skin to tingle; this silk, so fine and beautifully decorated, falls in a great swathe of elegance before me, for so far I have not sought to lift it and tie it about my waist. I would rather enjoy its full length and glide about here, my arms outstretched. There is no one here, no one at all, and perhaps the beauty in my lonely existence (for I do find beauty here) lies in these strange and curious fragments of time, fragments in which I encounter something I did not know before. I would not choose to be so alone, that much is certain, and the true shapeshifter makes use of the neighbouring room down below, and comes and goes, and is no friend to me (though, so far, neither is my enemy), and so, I am entirely alone, in essence, and must make the best of this.

The rain flushes in from the sides and torments the floor below, and up here, like a small nested bird, I hide from it, wrapping myself in fine feathers.

I listen out. I hear the storm afresh as it rounds upon this place, loud and weighty.

No use at all to think of paper, notebooks. The journal. Prototypes... I can only hope that the storm has not been broad in its reach, and that it has not touched my family. I hope my dear friend, Shizuka, is safe. The local people hereabouts. And Cat.

And still, the rain.

Beguiled by this long robe, I have decided to try some others. They slip easily onto the shoulders, and I observe how comfortably they rest there, how each of them moves. The subtle weight of the sleeves. I dance, barefoot. The textile rolling in the shadows. Afraid of the storm damage down below I know I must keep busy until it passes, and so I lay out each kimono with care, and have decided to study them more closely. I have never seen, nor cared for anything as fine as these, and find myself filled with all kinds of emotions. I dress up as though I am a child at play or an actor, but am neither. I sit cross-legged awhile in this fresh green gown and I am overwhelmed; filled with an easy and tender happiness. Decorated with scenes from springtime, I read this gown just now as though it is a book, tracing its story along the hem, adding myself in as a player in one of the scenes, wishing myself the young man lying beneath the tree; pale blossom in the air, people picnicking, drunk and laughing beside a river, silver blue; children playing, running in jade and yellow grass, teasing, dancing. Rainbow bubbles hover in the air.

I will wear this green gown longer.

I peer down to the floor below; still the water builds. I am at sea, and this typhoon blows itself in at quite a human

91

level, attacking from all sides with lashing rains that force themselves through low-lying windows, squeezing through walls. So far, it has not been eager to crash in from the top and I hope this does not change or the roof will surely give out. And the walls, though they swell and lean, *somehow* they stay put, and we sway and moan together.

I knew an even greater typhoon in childhood. Or so it felt. The local river burst its banks. The flooding was immense. I remember just how quickly we were ankle deep in mud-water right inside our house. I splashed about in it. I will not do that here. Then someone took charge, and quickly I was swept up in their arms, brought to a dry place, a safe place. We ate rice cakes. Or perhaps, that's misremembered, perhaps I added that afterwards.

When you are grown up there is so much to dread in the weather. And yet I realise I have treated this much as I would the weather of childhood. I have hidden away up here and done nothing more than rest and play. In truth, up here, it is a dressing-up paradise, and these robes have really been some luck. All I had wanted was not to feel cold. And I do not feel cold at all, but I have experienced something more, something of deep value, something moving, so to say, and these painted robes have filled my heart. I feel free in them, lighter in mood, joyful. I cannot explain it entirely, I cannot capture it well – something like dancing, something like being still.

I have returned the remaining kimonos to the appropriate drawers and hope that that will be enough to save them from this monster rain. The roof seems to be holding up very well. So far it is still the edges, the fringes of this place that seem most vulnerable. The rains drum away, but at no greater intensity than earlier, I can only hope the typhoon has done its worst by now and gains no further strength.

I have slept and heavily, and I wake to find my spring robes mopping up the rains. It's not good, but this kimono has served me well and kept me covered over as I dreamt. I cannot guess the time of day. I feel quite stiff. I stretch my limbs out slowly and am cautious as I look around. I do not know what I expect to see, but I know what damage a typhoon can do. The rains come again now suddenly, thick and heavy. Something has changed, the storm makes its attack from a new direction and with a different kind of rain. There are things that I should check on. I inch over to the top of the staircase, the waters have grown as I slept. I heave a great sigh, for I have not given a single thought to Cello, I am not even sure where she is. Guilt tightens my chest. I thought of nothing and no one when I climbed the stairs up here, and if I did it was only fleetingly. I wonder now about the shapeshifter. Can they survive big storms? Is it trapped in the room below? Drowned? Fallen asleep on the shelf and deep in slumber woken to a world of murky water, alone and afraid? And the temple folk. I wonder how they have fared.

I move away, I cannot go down there yet, it isn't safe. I take off the pale green robe, laying out spring in the hope it will soon dry.

I placed Cello in a cupboard some time ago, for sure I did – the thought comes back – and have not moved her since. I hope she might be protected there. And I hope the shapeshifter has a form that would save it, that it might swim out or climb and find some safety.

I have edged towards the window now, totally dark out

there, vast sheets of rain block out the light, and I may have slept much longer than I know. Truly, is it night again?

I had no chance to store away the prototypes, the paper ones. They will be ruined. What a lot of work that was … and all the coding … I am not sure I could remember it well enough if I had to start it over. No use to hold this thought. Sneezing and shivering, I look over the spring robe. I feel I cannot manage without it. And don't want to wear another. Damp and dirty, but dry enough at the top. I place it back around my shoulders.

I must stay calm. I will find a dry spot up here and lay out the other kimonos once again, perhaps just one at a time, and map the stories painted there in greater detail, for I must keep my mind occupied until this wretched storm has passed. I will trace the scenes along the robes, work at their meanings, and conjure a few more stories of my own. A quiet activity and that being the case I might listen out for Cat, and also for the shapeshifter. No matter what form it takes, if it has grown afraid, I must do what I can to comfort it.

10.

I have stayed up here much longer than I expected. It has been some days by now. I have not moved that much, my stomach is strange to me, deeply hungered. My mind, I sense has ruptured, or perhaps it is my spleen, there are pains, numbness elsewhere also, and I can make no sense of myself, body, consciousness, sanity. It does no good to notice. Perhaps I am dreaming. But I'm not. And awake I am so very lonely.

When I drag myself to look, the lower floor is muddied with a clay-coloured water, the smell is foul and dank. It is not all that deep anymore, but I will let the remaining water find its way out again before I venture there. In all honesty I have found it difficult to consider going downstairs at all. I have slept on and on, warming myself in the sun when it glimpsed through – a form of recompense somehow – and I have indulged in my new activity mapping out tales with the storytelling robes when I have lain awake, truly, the perfect distraction, for the devastation at ground level will be no easy thing to face.

When I woke again I found drinking water close by me. Not sure if I was dreaming I drank with heart and was glad of it. I was insanely dehydrated. And it occurred to me that perhaps I had been downstairs to fetch this, in a kind of sleepwalk – but the robe would surely betray this, it would be freshly wet and muddied, and if I had climbed down there naked, the stained waters would have left some residue, a tidemark on my legs. Ultimately, I can no more explain the water cup than the noodles I found on my return from the garden. I am grateful for both though they trouble me. And have I eaten something more, just very recently? More than anything I hope I have not been stealing again.

This lack of clarity surely points to the planting not having taken full effect quite yet. I might be less well than I realise. No hair still, but worse than that, these memory glitches, gaps, perhaps also misremembering; and really, no way to know if this is the case... Is it possible that my actions have taken on greater independence, overriding my conscious mind, that I am really not aware of what I do? I hope it's not that way. But how can you keep an eye on your behaviour and the state of your mind when you are so entirely alone? It is not good to be so removed from society, I see that, but I am still not fit to find my way back.

I have not heard the shapeshifter at all. I hope it is safe. I would be comforted at least by the idea of its return, for it would mean I was not entirely alone. It is all I can do to hope that it is well.

My thoughts, muddled.

Something else occurs to me, the very faintest sense of my head having been touched and by a hand that is not mine, for just now, as my fingers moved over my scalp, I was reminded of the touch of another. It cannot be a memory of my former girlfriend, Yumi, and nor could it be the fond and early memory of my grandmother's touch, for in both cases I had a full head of hair, and this was the touch, I might even say caress, of a hand that touched a head that has no hair at all. You do not feel the softness of fingertips through a thick head of hair. What you feel is wonderful, of course, but the sensation is entirely different when your head is smooth and bald. And I know it. It was skin on skin. A soft and caring hand drawn gently over my scalp. And not my own hand. Fantasy? Perhaps half awake my mind conjures this out of loneliness and desire. It is not real? But like the food and water that I can no more easily explain, it brought me comfort. If it is fantasy, then let it be, for I feel so lonely and my mind again becomes unstill.

And now I am troubled, for I borrowed the soil outside awhile, and I hoped to have treated the space with respect, and to have left it as close as possible to the state in which I found it. But now I don't remember. Did I make good the ground I laid my head upon? *Oh, what goes on with me, that I can never be quite sure?* I attempt to track back, but still I cannot speak for my actions with confidence. Oh, useless, useless head. I cannot think about it more. But I need to recover, and make recompense as soon as I am able, wherever there is need. It's not good to sense that you don't know what you are doing, that details are lost, perhaps even invented, that you no longer know what you are about, and that you are forced to accept that your mind might wander almost without you at times. Is that what happens? Does my mind just take a walk? Does it forget to inform me of my actions? What state is that?

Questions, and how they multiply! I have never questioned things deeply, and now I probe about and my curiosity takes itself off on journeys with a map all of its own.

I lost so much, was overcome with grief, was overwhelmed with self-pity, and the result is that now I am a 'thinking man'? One who now questions the world and himself? What a luxury. How selfish. For this to have been possible has required two specific things: the absence of work (in the formal sense at least), and the absence of time (without means of measure). I know for sure that my father would have seen this very differently, just the makings of a lazy, useless man. No work and too much time. How could that possibly equate to anything good or useful? But the world must have a place for minds to think, and it must permit the conditions that are conducive. But I am not a thinker, but rather, just a man who thinks, a guy who thinks where previously he did not. Things have shifted about, they have been shaken up, and a set of accidental circumstances have brought this about. Nothing more. And I have no idea if my thinking is of use, or if the mind truly wanders to no purpose. But a shift has taken place. Good or bad, I expect there is no going back.

I want to believe that the soil has nourished me. I planted a head and thoughts have grown. Is that what I intended? Farming myself, making something of and from myself, seeing what might emerge, what might evolve?

Well, perhaps so.

Simply watching a farmer does not make you a farmer, Takeo. You must do it for yourself. You must plunge your hands into the soil, you must dig and dig and dig, you must understand the weather like no other, you must know what you plant, what it needs, how long to tend it, how long to let it be, and you must appreciate the soil in which it grows. If you only watch, you will see but never do. My father's words somehow.

I am not a farmer.

I stayed the too-long hours at my desk, and so was made a salaryman. Fooled like many others that the part I played was something more, that one day my efforts would be recognised and perhaps rewarded. They were not, I was merely a cog. Easily replaced by any other. But I also gambled, and this made me a gambler. I took risks, but these I calculated, and I won. I am not a salaryman, and I may not always be a gambler, but I'm grateful for what it taught me. So many shifts in me, fault lines, tremors, but perhaps something good emerges also. Perhaps hidden fractures that with the right conditions reveal some unexplored zones. I cannot say, but notice I am animated suddenly. Before the planting, I worked at the prototypes like nothing else, failing again and again and again, but refining my skills, taking my time, solving the problems as they rose. And now I want to push on again in that way, and see where things might run. When the waters have truly drained away, I might have to start some things over, so to say, re-starting them, re-figuring, re-drafting them.

Well, I am far from being a craftsman, and there is no one here for me to study, and so I invent the methods on my own. I am a craftsman in prototype, a craftsman in the making. So arrogant! What happens here? But arrogance might just be necessary.

I am not a farmer.
I am not a salaryman.
At times I am a gambler.
And, in time, I will be a craftsman.

11.

Downstairs, finally the rainwater has gone. It leaves a dry clay-coloured residue. I sweep it from the steps. It covers the tatami and floor. The tatami are soaked through and will rot.

In the wake of the rough typhoon of my childhood that filled our home with mud, I remember my mother's extreme calm. I was dazzled by it, and I remember standing, watching her, waiting for tears, for huge, great tears. But she did not cry, rather, she was determined, and practical. She looked at me straight, and without words we heaved the tatami outside. Father would deal with them later. And we began, like all of our neighbours, to clean up our home. To clean up and get on with our lives.

The sun has come. It showers in as though with purpose. And all the brighter for its arrival on the back of a meddlesome storm. My mother also gazed at the sun that day, and drenched in a bright white autumn light, she was serene. It's gone, was all she said. Then she moved out of the sunlight and continued with the clean-up. That went on for days.

I see no other way forward than to adopt a similar methodical approach to that carried through by my mother. Back then I thought that the mud and dirt and dust would never end, that it could never entirely be cleaned away. But painstakingly we scraped, swept and heaved. I didn't mind the messiness that much in the daytime, I was a kid, but at night its presence felt so penetrating. It seemed to climb into my ears, crawled up between my toes, coated my feet, dusted my hair, and made my eyelashes twitch. And my eyes became sore. But somehow, finally, it was gone. Free of mud, new tatami arrived, and over time other spoilt things were mended or replaced. We moved on and did not speak about it.

I cannot readily replace the tatami, but the sun should dry them out if I position them well in here. But I sense I will not manage to clean this place as well as I would like, I am weak again, and now completely out of rice my body has begun at times to shake, but I will do all that I can.

I have checked the place over and find no sign of the shapeshifter's presence. I must assume it is safe for I lack the energy to worry. I have looked across at the temple and also at the temple dwelling and realise I did not need to be concerned. So fatigued and anxious I had forgotten that the other architecture is in a very much healthier state than this. Truly robust by comparison. I am content that the damage there will be minor. And the people there, surely safe.

There is a lot of damage down here, truly, it is a great mess. It is only luck that I had banished Cello from sight. And my cardboard stash is, for the most part, in reasonable order. Had I not recognised my lack of skill and set these boxes aside, and if I hadn't had the advantage of the plastic sheets, they would most certainly be ruined. There are damp patches on some, but overall they have survived well.

Those I used to practise on are a different matter, almost entirely destroyed. And the coding I had laboured over and inscribed with such care, now completely indecipherable. Stupid to think it could have been otherwise, but nonetheless I feel this more deeply than I would like. The coding, just gone.

Collecting these up it was as though something nipped at my flesh, and as I looked them over and took in the full extent of the damage, the scissoring effect on my skin, such as I felt it, only increased.

I squatted down on the floor awhile, lightheaded. Then came the sensation of slick paper cuts made to my skin. I did not know what caused it, I did not see anything, just a feeling, perhaps imagined. I passed out. When I woke my skin was covered in tiny blood markings. Insects had taken over the tatami in its damp and sun-warmed state, and bitten at me over and over. How quickly these things happen. I itch now terribly.

I forced the tatami up and pushed them outside on the temple side. And this I did without thinking, without a care of being seen. My body in a trembling state.

Over and again in endless repetition, I swept the place, but the dirt just re-emerged. Then finally, when I was truly and quite indescribably spent, it seemed to have gone.

The water damage would have to remain for I had not the energy to do much more. The spring kimono hung about my shoulders but by now was ruined. A deep band of clay and dirt blocked out the scenes as though troubled by a storm all their own. The little figures, houses, picnics under cherry blossom, all of them blotted out.

Ruined, I folded up spring and placed it by the door.

Desperate to stem the itching I tried to wash, and lacking food drank enough water to make my belly hurt. My muscles ached and were painful to the touch. My eyes were smarting and I grew concerned about my sight. My hands were often numb; and I was no longer sure of my hearing, perhaps that also failed. None of this was good. I climbed the stairs again. I took out a sand-coloured robe and curled up, a lazy cat in the cosy autumn sun. Soon, for sure, I had to feel better.

I don't know how long I slept, but I had the feeling again of my head being stroked. What fantastical events my dreams have become. My bitten and bloodied scalp experienced a caress so gentle, so very sweet and light, I am apt to believe that by taking up the position of a cat I suggested to myself the life of a cat, and so have been treated as such as I slept. The imagination is a powerful thing, my dreams seem now to offer some actual physical sensations, and as long as these are good ones I cannot find anything unpleasant in this.

There is a bowl laid next to my head. It is empty. I felt so glad when I noticed it and lent over expecting that it might hold food. I run my finger around the rim just now and taste it, there is a trace of something good. Hard to identify, but so long without flavours passing my lips this part at least makes sense to me. I know simply that what was there (for certain there was something) tasted good, perhaps delicious. And now what comes is just a very faint memory. I know that taste. Not well enough to name it, but enough to know that this is something that has touched my palate recently, and more than that, my stomach. Freshly rounded, but not bloated as from hunger or aching from the water, my belly tells me I have eaten. Then have I eaten whilst asleep? Is that possible? It seems that way. But there was no food in this place, none at all; I did not cook, and I did not hear anyone enter. How is it possible that I could sleep so very deeply that I did not hear a thing, then also ate and still did not wake? It makes no sense. My faculties are strange to me. My frame of reference shifts and shifts again just as the dimensions of the rooms in this place have so often shifted, at times altering my perception entirely, affecting my work on the prototypes and more importantly the models and my notes. I realise it cannot actually have been the house that altered, but some game played by my mind, but it has been so testing not knowing what I should trust and what I should not, and then dealing with all the extra work brought on by this confusion. A set of calculations some-times based on phantom walls, on shifting space. I would eventually find myself more fully conscious only to have to start over again with my work. The dimensions ought to have been so easy to calculate, truly the easiest part, but at moments I felt the rooms as though they swung about, the walls moving inwards or out, the inner walls shifting as though by themselves, the shoji swelling in parts or slicing itself up.

Too often I find the definite becomes indefinite, lines extend or else are truncated, and there is no way to check back, no way of knowing what can be relied upon. You cannot gauge density or proportion, obtuse angles sharpen and then soften; it suggests that what you see is entirely malleable, everything soft. The quality of the light shrouding detail at moments, accentuating, magnifying, even glorifying it at others. The light, it dapples certain areas, in others it highlights a surface, leaving the body of the object behind. Surfaces opaque, then translucent, stretch away and then are lost in darkness. What significance does any of this have? Are these surfaces, these objects, near to me or far? Do they change before me? When a mind is so unstill it is too hard to work things out. To lock things down.

But I must not doubt my work. I have to, and will, make a very fine box dwelling. The coding is lost, so I will simply master a new system, for there will be coding. What a strange burst of thought comes once the appetite is sated. What a simple being I am. An injection of nutrients or the warmth of the sun! Just like leaves. I am just like leaves.

I close my heavy eyes hoping to return to the dreams of a cat, to a warm caress. I lick my lips and curl up on the floor now in sand-coloured silk. I feel myself murmur, a strange form of self-comfort, a soft purr, and reach back into slumber. It's getting cold.

WINTER

1.

It is night-time and downstairs I hear movements. Perhaps it is the shapeshifter returned, its kindness run out, come to do me harm. Listening carefully it seems there is more than one. And they have voices. People. I curl up tightly as though I might not be noticed if anyone comes up here, so far no one has climbed the stairs and if they do I will clearly be seen. I am itching from something and it is hard to keep still. If I had the skills of a shapeshifter then I might easily assume a character that would have me escape this place or admit no particular attention. Wearing sand does not make you sand, purring does not make you a cat, and twisting and twitching draws attention.

The voices trail away. Return. Spiral up. I catch only fragments.

The sound of a foot on the first step below. Am I mistaken?

I catch my breath. This is the moment I have most dreaded. It brings on a fear that drains the life from you. The moment just before you are caught, before someone comes and finds you out. Once it is certain, once I am in their grasp, their hands clapped upon my shoulders, then it will be over, I can submit and take what comes, but the fear just now, it grips and shivers me. I twitch and twitch about. I must keep still.

But what will they do to me? They might have weapons and means of restraining the captive, though they have no need for I am quite unable to fight. But I should take action. If not to fight then to hide. I hope they won't beat me. By now I have slipped the last robes from the drawers, guiding them gently open, pleased they make no sound, and I have arranged the robes so that they cover me completely. I lie as close to the floor as I can. Nose, cheek, lips against the wooden boards. Perhaps I will be taken as nothing more than a messy pile of clothes. Laundry even. But I cannot breathe. I sweat covered over like this. And lately I have been alternately hot and cold as though I have fever again. What a mess. It's no good this way, I need at least to have my head uncovered, and underneath the clothing the sounds become muffled and I would rather not be taken completely unawares. What a choice I have: suffocated or discovered? It's no life to exist like this.

When they climb the stairs and find me, most likely they will fall back in fright, for I cannot imagine how revolting I must look by now. Malnourished, hairless, bitten over and bloodied (the bites did not heal well, there is scaring every-where and the scabs seem to catch on the smallest thing and bleed again); my body bruises these days at the slightest touch, I hardly recognise it as my own; and I am naked here save for this elegant female robe. They will detest me. And I? I will be driven forever from civilised society, cast out, shunned, and completely discarded. Utterly, most likely vio-lently, thrown away.

I doubt anyone would even bother to lock me up in a jail or put me on trial. This fine garment cannot hide its hideous contents. They will be sickened by my appearance and how I live, by what I am, and what they imagine me to be. For surely, this is disease? My crazed state, my physical weakness, my frightening appearance? People will be repulsed. They might even suffer some great ill effect simply from catching sight of me. I am certain that I would not be given a fair trial for the gathering number of things I might then stand accused of.

Indeed, I might be breaking more laws than I know. I have taken up residence without permission in a property that is not mine, I have paid no rent here; I have stolen from the temple; displaced moss and other elements within the temple grounds (to achieve the self-planting – but a matter not easily explained and likely to be read as deviant), and though my intention was to leave the place as I found it, I still think that perhaps I did not, disturbed as I was by Lightfoot; and, though I aimed to shore up this place against the elements, I failed completely and did not take the work involved seriously enough (though this is perhaps more a matter for my own conscience than the law, and I feel I could argue this point at least). Added to this, I have taken a full sack of rice in here and consumed it in its entirety; and helped myself to any number of things with regard to materials and my requirements for constructing the prototypes (which largely eclipsed my plans for fixing things – a measure perhaps of just how selfish I have become); then, I have helped myself to a bowl of ramen placed in here, and later some other tasty dish or perhaps dishes, casually assuming I had some right to do so, needless to say: without even offering thanks. However these things stack up, I am surely in all kinds of other trouble and am probably breaking all kinds of laws relating to my exit from society and the normal run of things – it always seems to be the case that when a person is missing, when someone finds himself ejected from society or else ejects themselves, that ultimately the police become involved, and when the lost are found it often appears as though a crime has been perpetrated. Perhaps it is also possible to break certain laws by accident, with no ill intent. Is any allowance ever made for this? Do courts show leniency with regard to such things? I don't have answers. And then there could be times when you find yourself quite out of your mind; somewhere very distant from the self you know and recognise, perhaps even hallucinating at certain moments, knowing not even which way is up, perhaps then further crimes are committed, again for which you had no intention or desire, and for which there is even no memory. What then? Or else the memory is temporarily tried, dimmed, muted. The knowledge returning only later. And because of this delay, whatever is said will have the appearance of being unreliable, made up, perhaps a calculated fantasy. Lies.

It is frightening to sense that you may have done something and have no sense of recall, no way to pull it back, no way to check over the behaviour, the actions, the movements of recent hours and days. It terrifies me. Brings me almost to a state of paralysis. And still it can all be the work of dreams. The trickery of sleep. But I do not know how things like this are played out in courts of law, or what truly happens to the dispossessed when they return, are found, and caught.

The dispossessed, they stumble along awhile and unless they swiftly reengage with the order of the world, their status is diminished and on their heads are laid accusations relating to so-called subversive behaviour, to strangeness and transgression, and these are then difficult, perhaps impossible, to deny.

I sweat.

I wonder, where is Cat?

Society evolves its perception of weakness, of poverty, of mental and physical ills and even something as simple as a 'run of bad luck', and like some host agent renders those troubled by such things as hostile and dangerous. It finds all those conditions and experiences interchangeable some-how. It grows the fear of them into something easy to drink, easy to assimilate and replicate. But the disease lies surely in the host. And is dispensed by it.

I know how I have regarded people I have seen living homeless lives, how badly I have thought of someone who has lost their job, and as for certain types of illness or those too low born to contemplate, I know I have harboured the feeling that their situation is simply a poor reflection of their character and perhaps also of their family. Put simply, they must have brought it on themselves. I have already stated that once I am completely well again, returned to myself, employed, properly housed, newly loved, yes ... once I have re-joined society in the full and proper manner, I intend again to shun all those I might have shunned before, for I realise that being part of civilised society is to do exactly that. Is that not the case?

Now my body shakes. And tears pour heavily from my swollen eyes. Truly, what is it that happens to me? Perhaps it is just the disappointment of finding I'm the man that I am. My heart so full of sadness, it swells ... aches. My head feels heavy and my thoughts are very complicated. I would rather have no thoughts at all than be stuck with these.

I fail, and I fail again. And perhaps there is nothing more.

2.

They are gone, the voices circling the rooms downstairs and the bodies that carried them. I am certain. I woke with a start to the sound of a door closing firmly and the remnants of warm chatter and sighs that slipped away into the temple garden.

My eyes are sticky, perhaps a mild infection. The kind known in childhood. I brush the drier parts away and worry how I could have let myself fall asleep while I should have been on watch. I do not know what I would have done had someone climbed the stairs, but I should have kept awake. I am not prepared for anything up here, except perhaps for dancing. What a mad old man I would appear to them, staggering about. Lucky that I was not found. I am so weak I could be knocked to the floor with nothing more than a stern look. And I am not convinced that I fell asleep but rather fell unconscious.

It is very cold now. I feel a stark shift in temperature, the air is different, and as I pull myself closer to the window I see that night-time has already changed into its winter robes. The sky and moon look so different as they move through the seasons; it looks misty out there just now, calm and misty.

If ever you experience the thought that you will not

make it through, that you might not live, then you must not let it settle. You should perhaps not even acknowledge it in case it should stick and take hold of you. Fortunately, I have not had such a thought, and for that I am glad. I am fine. Really, fine. I have things to do. I am a busy man with plenty to attend to. But before I can get started I must check what mischief has been done downstairs.

I have wrapped myself in three robes, placing one over the other for warmth, tied at the waist with a fine silk rope. This will do quite well and gives me the cheerful feeling that perhaps I am an actor or comedian preparing for a role. What a frightening sight my face must be, but I will imagine just for now that I am handsome.

I take the steps quite carefully, steadying myself as I go. Resting at a halfway point I consider how lucky I have been, so far managing to avoid being discovered. For I am truly fearful that had I been found I may have been restrained physically, perhaps even chemically, my arm strapped down, some terrifying substance shot into my vein. It's hard to know what happens to people. Behind the scenes. But here, I am. Still free. Free and busy.

Things have been changed down here. I take the very last step and am greeted by quite a spectacle. What has been done? New tatami. Fewer in numbers than I had before, but these are certainly enough and I like them very much. I step onto them lightly and in awe. Did I enter now a palace? Or do I step out upon the stage? What else? A nice plump futon. Something I did not have before. And blankets. I check just now and the old ones seem to have been taken away. I am aware also of a rather unpleasant odour. I know it. The smell of fuel. Kerosene. A row of containers, and in the kitchen more. And then I spy a box, a big one.

A brand new box. Well, I would have been happy to welcome such a fine-looking specimen even if it were empty, and I could surely find a home for it, and indeed, might make a home of it. It is the casing for a very fine kerosene heater. Perhaps the latest design!

I have so far only stroked and admired this heater for it seems my arms are too weak just now to lift it out, and I would rather not break the box but keep it completely intact. I do not yet know how I will use it. And the heater, it warms me just by the knowledge of its presence.

I sit a moment. My head is light. I need water. And had better bathe my eyes. I hope that when I have done so these new things will not prove to have been imagined. Sounds come. What's that? *Cat*. He is here. He mews. He knows me. I stroke his head but my hand feels tender and I have to stop. He is disgruntled but doesn't leave. He pads about and inspects the new items. He looks at me for an explanation. I have none, he turns his head and sniffs at the air.

I have moved to the window to check if anyone is there in the garden. Lights have come on about the temple, but I cannot see a soul. I cannot make sense of things. Why did no one climb the stairs and seize me? They know that I am here. They must. I threw out the infested tatami, and now they are replaced. And checking near the stove I have been delivered what can only be described as provisions. For I now discover a fresh sack of rice, all shiny and new; and there are vegetables. Hardy winter vegetables. I have scratched the surface of one and know them to be real. Surely, surely they are quite real. I grow emotional, somewhat sentimental. Unsure if I hear voices. Unsure of where they begin. In the head? Outside the head? Gone. And so, no matter. Best that I make myself busy.

I will cook a pot of rice immediately, for whilst I do not entirely trust my thoughts, my stomach will not lie. And once I have eaten I might have strength enough to set the heater going.

Cat has stayed. He watched as I set the rice to cook. And now that it is ready he takes a little.

I am caused to believe that whoever brought me these goods and supplies may also have been responsible for the ramen and perhaps the food brought upstairs as I slept. If this is the case, then it has to be temple people, perhaps their staff or some acquaintances. *Lightfoot*? Perhaps he has a brother.

This rice is so delicious, I can hardly believe the difference between the last of that old sack and these bright new shiny grains. If only there was some miso soup and pickles to accompany it, that would in fact be perfect. Pickles. I wish I had not thought of them. But the moment I am recovered I will drown myself in pickles. I will construct a vessel, large enough to contain my body and I will fill it entirely with pickles. I will roll about awhile and gorge, then lie back contented.

It is difficult to know if I am yet entirely mad, and then I speculate whether it might happen incrementally, and then I wonder if obsessing about pickles is a sign. But daydreams of pickles are surely the work of a healthy mind? Cat has gone.

So many things remain unanswered here. I half see and think I see. There are sounds in my head not always easy to ignore. And sometimes voices. Things shift, always 'sense' and 'no sense'. And always, everywhere, contradiction. I have been certain at times that what happens is the work of the shapeshifter, and then it is clear that people have been here. The arrival of these goods has to be the work of temple folk but the bowls of food are surely less easily explained. For I did not wake, saw no one. No note was left. And out of sheer hunger I still believe it is possible that I imagined these. But I eat the rice just now and am reminded of the fullness I experienced when I ate before, and the savoury flavours of the second dish come back to me. So, the food was real, the noodles and then the bowl of hotter-flavoured food; and was there more even? I find I can now identify at least that the last dish was spicy, spicy and delicious, though I do not know its name – but however these dishes came to me it was not by those who brought the tatami and other goods. The dishes of food were delivered by someone with a lighter tread. It must be so, or I would have heard them. This might imply Lightfoot, but I am adamant that it cannot have been him. I am also certain about the difference in the number of people and the tread of those who came, in fact, I feel confident about the weight of their steps to the degree that I would know them even if only one of them came here again. Whatever it was that brought the bowls of food was not the same as those who brought the tatami. I pick over the detail. Un-weaving, re-conceiving. And I notice a warmth of feeling, and find this activity rather a pleasure. I grow certain now that my impaired faculties finally begin to show signs of improvement, my hearing … yes, this freshly heightened sense being just the very first stage. Am I starting to recover, to rebuild, to reassemble? It's not easy to evaluate, but I feel that my hearing is now sharper than it ever was! And if it takes a while for the rest of me to catch up then I must rely on it where other senses still test me. The planting! Finally, it takes effect, it is so exciting to consider that this was not a waste of time. And far from being the ridiculous antics of a madman, it may have been an act that will yet prove pivotal in my recovery. Who knows, perhaps quite soon my hair will grow again. I move my fingers over my scalp and find it still bare. But to have my hearing restored, enhanced even, is plenty to recover my spirit just now. I must simply wait and see. Again, I had better keep busy, let things take their course.

I will try to wash and then I must look closely at the heater. I would like to cook the vegetables soon, but I shall not disturb them just now, they look rather beautiful there, lined up in a row. It is as though friends have arrived.

3.

It is a strange habit to have formed, but after any activity I find myself asleep again as though I have taken some special medicine for sleeping. I can only think it is the result of being in such a wanting state that makes my body capable of so little and for such short periods of time. And there is nothing to do but accept it. Outside any usual social order, there is no one here to chase my tail and no one's tail that I might chase. I live here inside a house which is falling apart, inside these fragile walls, beneath a suspect ceiling, beside some dismantled cardboard and a tidy haul of handy tools. A world of my own, and in many ways hard to fault. So I must take advantage of my deviant position. For really, it has many advantages. It fills me often with a sense of mischief and this sensation is worth a very great deal. It is an inside-house liberation. For within these walls, I dance to no one's tune.

After more fresh rice I climb the stairs once more. It's so cold now, but I cannot set the heater working despite my best efforts and so I make my way again to bed.

These poor kimonos are being treated so roughly by me. Still used as my bedding despite the futon and blankets down below, but I cannot bring myself to use them. So new and clean and bright, I have formed habits, and a brand new futon with its too white sheets is no place for a wretch. Returning to this upstairs room is now quite automatic, and so I slip inside my silken nest.

I feel safe up here. And I will take things steadily, not push too hard, but let my body benefit from the fresh food left here and allow it time to nourish me and make me strong again. And it is clear that I must set to eating in a pattern, with some consistency. It is surely the lack of this which often torments my mind. My thoughts always rush on when I have eaten, too great a contrast with the long spells without any food at all. Inconsistency becomes the order of things. My mood soars only to plummet soon after and then I struggle again to dig my way out. So, if I can finally overcome these erratic eating sprees, that might be for the best. It is wonderful, finally I have true supplies.

I cannot sleep, I will go downstairs and set about filling the heater. How difficult can that be? It is only a heater after all. It cannot beat me.

Since the arrival of all the goods down there it is my hope that if I try to behave as other people do, normal people, people in houses, that if I mimic them, and the rhythms of ordinary daily life, then perhaps I will begin to feel a little more like them, indeed, appear, more like them. For that is the aim. To re-join the normal run of things. I shiver.

The steps creak as I press on them. My mind flitting again, here, there. Too much thinking and suddenly I don't know what I am about or what I am doing. I cannot shake it. I came down here with a purpose, now it is lost. I touch my head, but it will not yield ... will not deliver whatever was my aim just now. At first there is the casual thought, it wanders in and settles as though it is nothing more than a polite visitor, but then it starts to fidget, to wander about, it makes itself too familiar, it behaves too roughly, and before long it's out of control, spawning other thoughts, smashing about the place, challenging, rebelling, forcing things up and out, unsettling my world.

I take myself upstairs again unsure of what I had wanted, surely nothing important. But I grow so very cold. Activity, that is what is lacking! Before the storm I was busy with the prototypes and planning, since then there has been a great deal of disruption and I am yet to settle back to my happy routine. The work on the paper boxes had a good effect. Repeatedly I came up against the most ferocious problems, but it was truly a joy to fathom them out. My fingers quickly grew stiff and how they would ache after too much careful work, but this is the pain of the craftsman, for I am by now at least something of a craftsman. Surely? And so such pain is almost a pleasure to endure. I make it sound romantic? Well, so it is. So it is! And a man must be busy.

I did not check before but it occurs to me that I did not notice the thin paper prototypes anywhere downstairs. The bulk of the practice cardboard, yes, that was truly destroyed, but I did not see even the remains of the paper ones and their bamboo struts... I can't remember exactly what else I threw out along with the tatami, the capacity of my short-term memory shifts still by extremes. *But how have I not looked for the little paper houses before now?* I remember at least that I was sorely upset by the damage to the coding and box material, so perhaps I did throw them out. Without a thought. Some automatic action. The failed precursors. I suppose it would not matter so much if that is what I have done, I am largely resigned to starting afresh. But even so … it would have been useful to study them, even damaged. Oh it troubles me now, for this project has become so important to me. I suppose, secretly, I have always held the desire to make something, to create something, to make of my life something useful. A young guy cannot just endlessly wave his hair about expecting to be admired his whole life through. Nice as it is, there is a limit to such activity. Really, I had no idea how important my hair was, no idea at all. What a big part it has played in my sense of who I am, in my sense of what it is that matters. But it was such an easy thing, a manifestation and statement of youth. It took no effort and afforded me great attention from childhood to manhood. So easy. Much too easy. Well, it's gone now, and my job has gone. The handsome salaryman. That time has gone. But what remains is my ambition. An ambition for life. For I believe (though current appearances may try to contradict), that my life is on my side. My aunt taught me that. Always to believe that life is on your side. I cannot say that I grappled with this idea in any deeply philosophical way, I did not. I was not a thinking guy. And I am glad of that. I simply took the words to my heart and treasured them. I knew my aunt's words would be true. Enough, or too much sentiment will seep in and surely weaken me again.

I have ambitions. Box dwelling ambitions. Wonderful box dwellings, useful places of shelter for times when a person is ejected from society, or when the weather and nature challenge people in ways it's hardly possible to conceive. With that in mind I must try to find the prototypes, the paper ones. You cannot simply abandon part of the process and, if nothing more, they will be impetus for improvement!

4.

A smell rises from the floor below. An aroma. Cooking, and not by me. And it rises from a dish that must surely be delicious. I take the steps with caution and pause at the bottom. Someone is here.

I need to think, and time to breathe. I have slipped into a shadow beneath the stairs. I make myself ridiculous. But whilst I accept that those who made the delivery of goods are most likely to be people with kind hearts who bear me no malice, it is just still possible that they do not know of my existence, and if I am discovered it could easily mean trouble. I have been happy to assume that these things were left here for my use, but why? They may well have been put here for someone else. Someone yet to arrive. That makes more sense. *And are they here now? Just arrived!* It could be that someone comes to stay here, and to facilitate this, provisions have been left in readiness. In preparation. *And so, is it them I hear just now?*

Sounds. There is certainly someone in the next room. What an idiot to have allowed myself to think of this place as mine. Always delusion. A sign of insanity? If nothing more, then a further sign of my being here too long.

I realise I still cannot readily gauge things well, cannot draw clear lines or markers, cannot reliably peg, divide, isolate, cannot *know*, the real from the phantom; but then at other times I have experienced great clarity of thought, I have been certain of things. Certain I was recovering. But was I right? Could my conviction about clear-sighted moments also be flawed? Are there simply degrees of hallucination, dreaming, imagining, wrong seeing? Perception might be something that is always negotiated, recalibrated; its provocations carefully noticed if you are able, moderated where necessary, where possible. Where possible…?

There is movement in the next room. My heart beats fast. Knowing the rightful person is here intensifies the fact that I have no right to be here at all. Vile perspiration hot on my skin. The salt from the sweat, in my eyes now. Outstaying my welcome? *There was no welcome! You were not welcome to stay here! You had no right!* I wipe my eyes. My legs tremble. What I am doing here?

Something just happened. Noises through there. Other noises. They are aware of my presence? They know I am near. I have sucked in my breath so tightly but this is a mistake for when I breathe out I will surely make some deadly sound, gagging for air.

I don't know if I said those words aloud. I have put my hand over my mouth to prevent more. It is a strange sensation, as though the hand is not mine. As though I disassemble. Like a puppet, all sticks and cloth. Or perhaps the hand is really someone else's. But there is no one by me. The hand is mine. Tears fall, they settle like glass drops upon my fingertips and slip around my hand. And now a greater sound comes. Scratching and dragging; and now creaking. The small window through there as it opens. I know that sound from before. I want to look, and my heart beats so fast as though it might implode. I never think of my heart, never perceive it to be a fist-shaped chunk of flesh inside my chest – but now I see it. But not as a fist. Not as a bodily organ. Just a small, thin and hungry mouse upon a bicycle, an old and rusty bicycle, and the mouse is pedalling as hard as it can, only just now it makes little progress. In my mind's eye I see nothing more than a mouse. Come on, I say to it, keep going, I try to encourage it, but it seems so tired. Quite worn out. The sounds drift away. I hold still.

Now a scuffling sound. I keep myself still. And silence. I wait some time. Nothing more just now. I feel certain I am alone again. I tread carefully and push the door. No one. But the row of vegetables has been disturbed and there is a pot on the stove, tantalising steam rises.

I creak the window to check the sound again. There is no other way out of this room save for the one door and no one passed me. I cannot say for sure, but now I more fully sense it was the shapeshifter. It must have been. There was certainly no person in here. Whatever it was left through that window, and it would not readily admit a person, except perhaps a child, and this was surely not a child? It could have been an animal, but that does not explain the cooking. It has to have been the shapeshifter, taking on first the body and movements of an animal that might easily enter this place, then assuming human form once in here. But still I can say nothing with certainty.

It has been both benign and illusive, for I would have expected to notice patterns emerging even without much conscious effort. Most things are creatures of habit, and routine comes no matter how hard you resist. Perhaps that begins to happen just now. For isn't there an overlap between my suspicions of the shapeshifter's presence and

the arrival of food? Savoury dishes that I cannot easily identify but which always offer up the most appetising smell? It
seems there may be some crossover. Pure hypothesis for the
moment for the incidents with the food are surely too few
to draw conclusions from: the first was ramen which I know
perfectly well, but at other times the food has been far more
rich and spicy. Is it possible that the same being brought a
very common dish and at other times more exotic food?
Could be. It is also true that though the ramen was placed
down here and seems less obviously to have been brought
for me, the tastier food was most definitely positioned close
by upstairs while I slept and can surely only have been left
for me. What to make of it? Was the ramen intended for
someone else? No one arrived and complained, and yet the
empty bowl was removed. I can't find good answers, but
my interest is piqued. And so, what next? I am drawn to
the stove, but the food doesn't seem quite ready and I've
disturbed things here. Did I frighten the shapeshifter? I have
too often felt a paralysing fear since my exit from society. I
can't bear to think I have induced fear in someone else, but
I can't fix this just now. I'll turn off the stove for safety and
leave the ingredients where they lie. If I withdraw, the
shapeshifter might return. I will leave the window as I
found it. And there is nothing more to be done in here. I
must deal with the heater and search for the prototypes.
Although, better not to do that right now, the sound might
keep my friend away. I should go quietly upstairs and busy
myself there. Or simply rest and make no sounds, then it
can return and feel unchallenged. I will check again and
see if it has been here when night falls. Darkness eases
things, collapses the space, renders it neutral. And I like the
quiet of the dark. Without limits. Space without walls.

5.

I have tried to spy on the visitor, but still I have not seen a soul. And the activity inside the kitchen has been cleared right away. Up and down the steps I have travelled numerous times and over some days by now, but nothing. I begin to wonder, in slender lucid moments whether the shapeshifter is in fact invisible, for never do I see it! Or does it drug me? There is again the residue of something that has crossed my palate, and still I cannot name it. I sleep so long, and it makes no sense to me. Close to drunkenness, my head heavy, thoughts in some altered state. And then there is the matter of my belly, warm and full. Can a man be so exhausted just from eating? And it seems, I have been eating … eating and eating. Dishes arrive and are removed. But I see no one. How to explain this?

And despite good food and rest my limbs feel heavy, weighted down. At times they shake, or tingle, or else there is a loss of sensation. Several times I have fallen down the stairs. I have passed out, then found myself stricken – a kind of demented confusion. Nothing seems to cure me. It has really been a very long time by now, hasn't it? Since I entered this place? And also some good while since the planting?

And there are other strange happenings here. I notice the warmth rising from downstairs. I go downstairs to turn off the heater for safety only to find this already done. I cannot lift the kerosene canister to top it up, but this also happens without me. I notice the gauge, half full, then full. The life around me takes on an automatic quality. I eat and rest, but ultimately I question less. What use? What need?

Nothing bad happens. I take the steps back upstairs, curl into a ball and sleep. I think of Cello. I have not seen Cat. I descend again. Heat on or off. And then return once more to my kimono bed.

In a moment of stillness, I try to settle and accept the time it takes to get well. And though I do not see the shapeshifter, in some half-conscious state I sometimes sense its presence and have grown to feel quite comfortable with this, and its clever, almost silent activities, its agile moves, its ability to morph into whatever shapes it makes and remove itself in just the nick of time.

By now it no longer unnerves me to find things altered or moved about, the leaving of meals and the removal of empty dishes. If I hear the shapeshifter's sound it is always one that is withdrawing, fading, and I, again, halfway to sleeping. The visitor, it seems, aware of my rhythms; and I, untroubled by theirs.

The door to the shapeshifter's room remains closed, but I leave it that way. I am full of contradiction. I want to find the shapeshifter, to see it, to introduce myself perhaps, and yet, while all is well, and still I am rather weak, I see the sense in letting it be. Am I a fool? But I know what anxiety is caused when you fear you might not be alone, or are about to be found out, that trouble might come, and so I will endeavour to let it alone, as though I am here, but quite as though I am not here. That a certain atmosphere of calm prevails. Lightfoot does not have a monopoly on serenity. He can make that temple and gardens as tranquil as he likes, but wait and see if I cannot achieve the same in here.

6.

The house sways and moans, still smarting from the typhoon. I might have been swallowed by a whale the sounds it makes, and around me, waves of darkness. Sometimes the noises soften, and House seems to murmur, satisfied, as though she too has eaten something warm.

Well, I have missed my work a very great deal, and though I fear the loss of the paper prototypes, it is time to know, time to see if I might find them. If they are anywhere, they are in a room downstairs.

As I enter each space, I am made to feel a stranger here. I become the trespasser once more. It is darker than I expected, I don't seem to know this space. The dimensions were not these, were they? It must be right, it was always like this, I suppose, or I confuse this room just now with another?

This door creaks so fearfully, you might expect the ceiling to fall in. Straw and clay fragments give way. I had better go about my search with great care.

Moving, as I have, between just a few particular spaces I have mostly felt that I am in a much smaller house (though I know full well that it is large), and it seems that in doing so I have reduced the place to a size and atmosphere that has suited me rather well. The rooms I have occupied have been my friends, and these other rooms seem alien to me. Mere acquaintances, and we are yet to know one another in any useful sense. Naturally I have entered these other rooms at least once before in order to check what was there and to be certain I was alone, but I have generally withdrawn again. What would be the point in spreading myself out? I am just one man. I need to wash and eat, to rest and work. And I have come to think it is just an extravagance to take up more space than is necessary.

In a room by myself, I might only be temporarily alone – for it's as though someone might join me at any moment – but in moving from room to room to room there is clear evidence that there is no one here but me. Not a good feeling for such a protracted length of time. Better that I focus on the task, mindful of the fragile timbers here. The ground has experienced some minor quakes lately, but so far House only rumbles and growls.

I check another room now. This so utterly dark, a solid darkness, and my eyes grown tired, I had better bring a candle.

I return, and my eyes settle now upon a canopy of fine white lines, the candlelight catching them, a map, a weaving, of linked edges; and pale, quivering panes of frost-like paper. The prototypes. They're here…

It is fair to say my heart is dancing. The small mouse has stepped off the bicycle. The wheels spin by themselves awhile, the mouse takes a bow.

I must be careful with the candle, and for once I wish that time would play a useful part and that daylight would come that I might see them much more clearly. I did not leave them here. I check back inside my mind, I don't recall this move. I stored the boxes away, and Cello, and much later, after the typhoon, I know and can remember that I moved the tatami and only the tatami outside. But I did not move these.

They seem to have been arranged. They have been given a kind of creative ordering, a scheme has been imposed. It's not my work. Placed so carefully like this, the little prototypes have the appearance of something most impressive, perhaps a sculpture. What a thing. By candlelight, the panes are lit in places, and the light then runs along the edges, as though a continuous outline. No, I did not do this. I did not arrange them in this clever way. Not even for a moment would I entertain the idea that this is something I had assembled in my sleep or in some fitful moment when I have been unwell, perhaps out of my mind from hunger. Not at all. I would know if this was my work. It belongs to someone else.

The mouse pirouettes just now as though he is accomplished in ballet. I have put my hand to my chest to calm him or quickly he will find himself completely tired out.

What a wonderful thing. The precursors presented here in all their glory. What resilience they have shown. And how cool they look. Someone saved these little works of mine and then arranged them so. An act of care. I am baffled that they were not considered rubbish. Well, they are found. They are found, and soon the new work can begin.

I will check them over more thoroughly when it is easier to see. I would like to get back to work on these as soon as possible. The mouse pedals the bicycle some more, and is truly overexcited. I take a breath. Really, this has lifted my spirit enormously, but I must keep myself steady. I take the candle, close the door, and leave the prototypes to rest.

I put out the heater as I go for it is nicely warmed in here. I would like to lie down just now on this fresh new futon, pull the blankets close about me and sleep and sleep and sleep. But I cannot. Still, my poor body and that too new bed, we do not fit. I will climb the stairs and lay again in my kimono bed. I have made it my nest, and like a dog I turn and turn until I find the perfect spot, until I am warm and covered over, until my rough bones are cushioned against the floor. A man like a dog. But it suits me well enough.

If I wake I will listen out for my friend downstairs. And something nice occurs to me just now. That if the shapeshifter finds the need, it might make use itself of the futon and the blankets. I hope it would. Perhaps I should have left a note down there. Can they read? Perhaps it will sense my presence in my usual place, and realising that I am perfectly content this way, will happily take up the fresh new bed without permission or enquiry. I hope so.

Well, I still cannot truly answer for the arrival of all those new things. But since no one has come to make a claim on them, I see no reason why we shouldn't make use of them.

I have laid myself down, and suddenly I ache, every single part of me, and in a terrifying way. What is it? Pains shoot through my flesh and bones as though I am being spiked beneath some great machine or laid upon a bed of nails. My body is stiff, and in some involuntary action I have thrown off the robes, I cannot move, and there is no way to retrieve them. I am so cold. Stricken with something. *I don't know what this is...* I have tried to call out, but there is no sound in me.

There is snow outside the window, falling.

7.

There is a blanket over me. I do not recognise it. It is soft and light. But now, as I move, I find it heavy. I hold still as thoughts run ahead of me as though viewed on a screen.

The screen is suddenly blank, it seems I have shut my eyes but I touch the lids and my eyes are open. It is my mind then that closes. I know that this has happened before, and when it does everything seems lost. You are presented with a very particular darkness, and plummet as though down a deep and empty shaft. And each time it happens you feel so very afraid. Of everything.

It lifts momentarily, and I can't measure how long the episodes last, but when they come I am so filled with terror that even the most fragmentary exposure feels like some protracted sentence. As though a criminal left in a cell without light or windows I wonder has it been moments this way or days?

I try again to move. No good. I try to focus on a single easy thought. But now I cannot find words. Cannot find the *right* words. I feel them scatter, then they are gone altogether. I don't know if I have lost them and perhaps later I will recover them or if they have left me altogether. More and more I feel words edge away from me, gaining confidence as they go. A troupe, travellers, a line across a sand horizon, and they look back but briefly over their shoulders to bid me goodbye. I can see them, in the distance, and how they chatter as they leave. I hope they come back soon.

I lie here, a scraggy bird with broken wings. I move my lips as though to speak but nothing whatever can he beard. The house creaks, and so I am sure that still I have my hearing. I have the fear that this house will yet lose its might and tumble down on me. And truly, I could not call for help, I cannot speak at all. Perhaps it does not matter. In any case, this house seems to have survived so much already, it must remain.

I can barely remember the last time I spoke with anyone.

Not even who it might have been. And if someone was here I would not have anything important to say. Is that why the words have gathered themselves and taken themselves away? Perhaps sensing they're not needed? What a sorry situation. Well, I do not have to care.

I am glad of the blanket. I expect it was the shapeshifter that brought it here. It might have been Lightfoot, but my instincts tell me not. That he is light on his feet suggests merely that he is not easily heard, it tells you nothing of his character, and I see no reason to attribute him any great acts of care. He is a monk, of course. But so what? It does not make every kindness his. I'm not so naive to think that being a monk makes a man a good man. I am a good man, am I not? Or at least, not a bad man, or not a very bad man, and certainly not a man with bad intentions, and I am no monk. I am just an ordinary man. Very ordinary. That's all.

I drive myself insane this way. What goes on? First the fear that words desert me, that I will be left here an empty man, just a skin, paper thin on brittle bones, a mind entirely lost, no organised or intelligible thoughts to be found; and then, in a flash, I feel besieged by words that form themselves into thoughts that cause me nothing but trouble. Torment. Most of them nonsense.

If I could calm myself, if I could eat well again. Have I been fed? I don't remember. Perhaps by now I should keep note, yes, I should write it down since I clearly can't recall. That's the only way to have routine. I have checked beside me, but there's no food and I can barely move. I'm afraid to sleep or even close my eyes too long for fear this terror will trap me in dreams once more. To alleviate this I have been staring, hard as I can. The eyes must not succumb to the downward motion of the lids or they will soon give in to the *slip, slip* into sleep, a terrifying sleep, and I cannot take more nightmares.

The long staring causes muscle pain about the eyes. I bear it. But still I wish my bones did not feel this way, so heavy, as though in chains held to the ground. Truly, if all I can do just now is lie here then I will need to empty my head. In fact, rather than worrying myself that words are leaving me I must in fact encourage them to go! I must tip up my mind as though a water jug and empty it completely.

If only I could stand again upon my head. I think that might help. But my limbs are dead weights. I cannot raise a hand. I was so proud of the planting. But again and again I have to push out these sorrowful thoughts.

If I cannot empty my head as swiftly and efficiently as I would like, then perhaps if I allow the thoughts to become sufficiently trivial then they might simply trickle away.

I think again of Lightfoot. It could be him that helps me with food and supplies. I know it. But I cannot bear the thought that it is him. I have seen how he parades about in his elegant robes, with his twinkly eyes, and his neatly shaven head, so handsome that way, and I, so ugly ... *serene* is truly how he is best described, so serene that I cannot stand him. Why should he have the sort of head that looks handsome when it is so closely shaven? Why should his forehead be so broad and tall as though to suggest to the world some great intelligence deep within, some inherent wisdom; some ferocious, though seemingly subtle, charisma? I am not sure that any of these things are appropriate traits for a monk to display. They seem manipulative, filled with vanity. I admit that my original reasons for disliking him were entirely irrational, but now it is clear that I should neither like nor admire the man. He's a fake, an imposter, a phoney. It might even be the case that I am more naturally suited to his role.

It seems no food is left here in the past long while.

There is no one here.

I can smell the snow in the air as it moves there outside.

8.

Finally, I have edged my way over to the top of the steps, I see the futon and the blankets. The futon still not slept upon. The heater, off. A breeze moves up here and with it the delicate scent again of fresh sweet snow. It tickles. My heart swells, a tear warms my cheek – I would snowboard and ski when I was younger. Living close to the mountains it was easy, and the older guys would laugh at the Tokyoites paying tons of cash to go there and do the same, strutting about in their cool shades and bright gear. But I wanted to be like them. I wanted to live in Tokyo and take those short breaks up in the mountains. I envied their image: *so cool*, and the pace: *the faster and faster living* … I wanted urban life so much, I hungered for it, every single thing about it. And then I became them.

Back in my hometown I always knew if the snow was coming from the scent in the air. My Tokyo co-workers laughed when I told them that I could sense and smell the snow, they found it pretentious, and thought me too much the 'country boy' just as Yumi's father did. It doesn't matter. I can smell snow when it comes, that's all.

It feels so strange lying on my too-thin belly here, peering over the steps and down to the floor below. I had hoped to find the futon slept upon, the blankets left messily, a sure sign of a happy sleep and someone having woken hurriedly to go about their day. And perhaps I hoped to witness someone or something still there, maybe the shapeshifter deep in slumber. At some stages I am sure it has adopted some feline form, its slick and agile movements seem to suggest something like that, entering by that long slim window, resting on the shelf. And I thought it could relax more with the comfort of the futon, but it could be shy I suppose, or too polite? And perhaps they do not rest. Their lives ever shifting, maintaining a state of high alert, ready to shapeshift at a moment's notice, to escape danger, to move swiftly in whatever task they have in mind. But truly, I feel so disappointed to see the pure white surface there, a bed not slept upon. I am so terribly lonely. I would so like to have a guest, *no*, I would LOVE to have a guest, a friend come to stay. Well, it seems I dragged myself over here, and for what? I grazed my belly on the way, and now I cannot get back and lack the strength even to turn myself over! *If I could just ... turn over!*

I feel the framework of a memory, someone turning me, perhaps rolling me, onto my back, then losing consciousness, waking, finding that I lie upon my nest again. I am made to sip something.

I am in a room inside a very large house, a new house, made of fresh pale wood. I can smell it. The sliding doors move and close in on me in a snap. I grow afraid. I feel myself pull back and they push open and wide again and the scene behind them changes. Summer. The doors open up to   gardens. Gardens I have never seen. The sun beats down on me and warms my face. I am myself again. A self I recognise. My hair is thick and glossy, my skin is smooth and warm and brown as though I have been out in the sunlight for many days. My nose is shiny, it tickles. I am wearing a white robe, thin like paper, fine like silk. My heart beats at a happy rhythm, a contented mouse, the bicycle running well. It starts to rain and I am thrust inside again, the doors move in and out making a slapping sound as they meet. It startles me. The wheels run on alone.

The frames of the doors are dark now, the house is an old house, it all closes in and I cannot fathom the dimensions. I am sitting at a desk trying to calculate the space I occupy, the space I need, the smallest space I could take up, for the sense I have is that I take up too much space, that I have no right to stay, that I cannot reason or negotiate this, and finally – that I have no right to occupy even this small area, that I have no right to occupy any space at all.

9.

Semi-conscious, I have found my head tilted towards a bowl of something warm and sating, I lay back again, and then I take some more, and each time my head has been supported by a hand that is not mine. And I have, at other times, felt my head caressed again and by the same hand. Sometimes I sensed a familiar smell, not the food this time, but something else entirely, the smell of another human being. I feel that I recognise their smell but cannot place it. I also know that this is not possible. No one knows me, or knows where I am. A tear slips across my cheek. Someone smooths it away. The scent comes again and is accompanied by a voice that makes a warm shushing sound, the kind that people make for babies when they wish gently to encourage them to sleep. It has a soothing effect. I cannot move, I cannot see anyone, but I sense it is a woman's hand that touches my face. Or perhaps I simply wish it so.

I must have slept or passed out again, I cannot tell. Perhaps it is overstating it to say that I am passing out, but that is how it feels. I re-emerge and each time it is a sweet reprieve from terrifying darkness. Then, too soon my weighty eyelids draw down on me and form the doors to some ancient fetid jail. I can remember at least that this has not always been the case. I am aware that I do not normally think about my eyelids nor any other part of me so often. I realise now that the body makes itself known most boldly when it is in distress. I am forgetting, of course, the case of vanity, for we also consider our bodies overmuch in moments such as those, but that might also be categorised as sickness. How could I worry so long and so deeply at the loss of my hair? A man does not die from this. He does not feel pain, and any discomfort really is minor, not much more than the chill of colder weather (for I am conscious of how much warmer my head was during the winter months when I had hair). Aside from all of this, Lightfoot even manages to make baldness a fine and handsome look. What a pitiable man I am, so long troubled by such a trivial happening. I have indulged this. We have no great need of hair; it is hardly like losing a limb or your eyes. And at times I might have dashed out my own eyes to dismiss the terror they have seen.

That soothing sound comes again, and the hand upon my head. I wonder if I have been shouting out in pain, for at times the pain is at the level of insanity. I cannot tell if I call out. Still I cannot monitor myself in the normal, automatic way. I hear my voice and think it exists only in my head, but perhaps it is audible. If someone heard, it could unsettle them enormously. The ramblings of the mad.

The gentle shushing plays on. It feels like the edges of waves and they lap over me. I feel drawn to notice the sound, to give in and quiet myself.

Quiet.

Slow, slow.

Quiet.

A hand upon my head.

Though I had pushed against the sense of containment and limitation imposed by time, I notice the rising sun, the night as it falls and I find comfort in them now. I place them in my mind alongside the small activity that happens here and feel I can begin to measure out stretches of time and become aware of myself beside it. It seems to allow me a place, it makes me exist as though I am in relation to it, as though an aspect of a plan, a scheme, a point on a grid, and it gives me a sense that I am real, for when you are too long alone and away from the world you slip into wondering, between moments – sometimes just 'flashes' – of clarity, whether you exist at all. To dissuade yourself of thoughts as terrifying as this, you have to find a way of placing yourself in this world; and time, however ugly, however filthy to the touch, and odorous, is useful in this.

In the last days, I have noted things in greater detail and held them in my mind, and I believe I have done this for longer and longer periods. It is hard to be certain, but I notice a shift. It seems that at the same time each morning my head is carefully lifted and I am eased awake – and I have been caused to wonder if I would wake at all were it not for this gentle encouragement. When I am woken I feel a clean, damp cloth moved with care about my face. I cannot express just how tenderly this is done, but when it is over I feel as though my skin is new. It is a fresh and alive kind of feeling as though I am a turtle hatching into the world, the shell that very moment broken through.

The stickiness about my eyes, which lasted such a very long time and must have been an infection, has now quite gone. The surrounding eye muscles no longer ache and that is also a relief. I am given water once my head is raised. I lap like a kitten, and though someone must see this I have the sense that no one sees, and so am quite at ease. I am given food, in small amounts, of various kinds, always soft and easy to take. And in between each careful action, again and again my head is held or stroked or covered by a cloth. I imagine the cloth is placed there for warmth, to keep off the worst of the winter chill, and it works quite well. I have a rich feeling of gladness at those moments, and once I have finished eating I drift easily back, often now, to a gentler kind of sleep.

At other times I become aware that I am being washed more thoroughly. I notice this especially when it is the turn of my feet because they tickle. The rest of my body seems not to respond in any normal way to touch, in fact I barely notice any sensation, but I suppose whilst being cared for this is a preferable state. And I cannot express how much I appreciate being clean. Really, you can only know what a luxury this can truly be when you have lain in your own sweat and grime for days and nights too long to count. If you add on whatever vile elements a body must emit when it is deeply sick, you might half imagine that it is the most cherishable state to find your body clean once more. It restores a modicum of self-worth, of pride, and it removes you from a darker place.

And so, with some degree of regularity, I find myself turned onto my side, then to the centre again of my nest and laid on my back, and then after some moments rolled to the other side. This seems to take place on two occasions. In the first case it is to wash me, and in the second it is to change the cloth beneath me. By now I no longer rest upon the robes but on some layering of cotton sheets. They lack the warmth of the silk, but it's no good to sacrifice fine robes just to make a bed for a sick man. I am gently patted dry, wrapped in a cotton robe, and finally covered over with blankets. There is even the hint just recently of some minor communication, and I am aware of myself emitting a kind of mellow grunting sound, sometimes with the intention of expressing that I am content and grateful, and at other times in a somewhat weak grumble (though I certainly do not mean to complain), but as though to indicate that an extra blanket would be welcome just now. I don't know why, but I am unable to speak in a way that I wish, in a way that is normal. Nicer words sometimes form in my mind but I fear there is a disconnection still; and I also fear I may cry out or ramble when I have not granted words permission. But I do not know for sure if this occurs, I simply sense an imprint, a shadow, so to speak, of words uttered that I did not intend. But I am guessing that I have not truly caused offence, for the one who tends me returns and makes no complaint of me.

I am aware also that the kerosene heater is used with greater frequency. Its smell is quite penetrating and a mild fog coils up the stairs. Despite being slightly unpleasant, the smell is welcome because it is familiar, and the gentle warmth is appreciated.

I cannot vouch for this, cannot assess it well enough, but sense that I have begun to feel a little closer to myself, as though on the edge of myself, close to the entrance, about to knock at the door, it is hard to describe, but I feel less afraid and less suspicious. And it is somewhat disconcerting when you have lived in a state of perpetual anxiety, and for such a long time, to notice suddenly that you no longer feel that way. The irony! And noticing that I feel 'something like myself' alerts me to the truth of the matter: that if I am something like myself, I am in truth still some distance *from myself, from him*, some way away from Takeo. What anguish. First, moving out of myself, and then back to my self... *And what is it anyway? 'Self'?* It is disarming to discover that it is so negotiable, malleable, so unstill. But this part, so to say, *the recovery, the recovering*, might be quite exciting. I try to take it that way. For it is in many ways a kind of metamorphosis. A rebuild. A refit. A cracking of a shell, the shedding of skin. It really could prove to be the case that I am still in development. No bad thing. Truly, the prototype of myself. Yet to emerge. When he comes, I hope he will have hair.

I make the casual assumption that I might still return to my former self, or recover as an improved self, a better version, but I cannot be sure that this will be the case. Perhaps

I will not. Perhaps I will only recover in part, some aspects, some percentage. Or perhaps it will be worse. Fragments. Patched up from junk.

I have no idea what it is that I have been suffering from. I believe by now it might have been several things, one even contributing to the next. And perhaps some damage is left, something permanent, or perhaps some symptoms linger, traces, like scars. I speculate how I would like this to end. I consider the possibilities of the better self. An 'other' self. Versions, types.

Takeo One: the prototype, the experimental version.

Takeo Two: a sick man, in transition, awaiting refiguring, revisions, rectification. Fine tuning, some perfect distillation. I might be recast, so to speak, for certainly my body has undergone some considerable turmoil. It would be nice to think that something quite reasonable might result from all this discomfort. Then I would look back on it and not mind so much. The idea that Version Three might emerge from the ruins of my former self becomes more and more exciting.

My cotton nest is coming undone. I had better lay still. I lie and watch a fragile light as it moves over surfaces whilst my face lies in shadow.

I must try again to capitalise on the moments of greater lucidity. I think of them as tiny raindrops falling separately, then gathering in number, bouncing into other drops, and finding themselves compatible, joining up in greater and greater numbers until the moments can no longer be singled out, and eventually I picture a small sea of salient thought ripple to the shoreline. What a joy it will be if this will be the case.

I feel the warm hand upon my head. I must have grown too animated. I am being cooed into a calmer state, and find I am helped now to sip tea from a bowl. Tea. A delight in itself. What happens? Never have I delighted in tea. Beer, yes, sake too, cold water also, never tea. New things happen to me. New sensations, appreciations. I feel happy as I drift once more into a deep and comforting sleep.

SPRING

1.

It is really something, to sense the recovery of health, or even the possibility of this, and I realise now that never having truly experienced illness before, it follows that emerging from it is also new to me. I have been finding it a strange and curious process. At times I am sure my condition has not been good at all. First a brutalising hunger, and then illness, disease perhaps as its companion, and in such a state you become aware of yourself as little more than matter, as no more than sinew and bone, and at times less even than these. You no longer feel whole, your thoughts set to roaming, detaching, splitting both from themselves and also from you, as though you could no longer claim to hold any particular thought or view as your own, as though ideas simply travel through you and 'you' are merely a portal; as though there is nothing to you and therefore nothing for them to attach to, and so, you, *you ... are what?*

When you are ill, you are less certain of things. That has been my own experience at least. Curiously, in some moments, I have found the uncertainty liberating, and have encountered thoughts I never had before. And this? It is a strange but brilliant high.

At present I have very few belongings in the normal sense, no relationships of any kind – due, in part perhaps, to my isolated state; and my thoughts are nothing special. So reduced, I become nothing, perhaps less. And yet, I find I do not really mind. I simply notice this, realise, observe it to be so.

As regards my physical health, it is wonderful to find the limbs that have been so heavy for so long are now happy to be raised up from the floor at least by the smallest degree, and I have, in fact, just raised my right foot high enough to see! I had almost forgotten what my feet looked like!

I have now just turned my ankle and made my foot move first one way and then the other in a vague half circular motion. It hurt a little when I stretched it out straight. A few happy tears come.

I have not been able to pull myself up to look about. I still cannot easily raise my head, and though this bothers me, perhaps some improvement comes there quite soon also.

But more than anything my mind is preoccupied by the identity of the one who tends to me. I hope above anything that this is not merely a phantom, that I truly am being fed, that I truly am recovering and that this current situation is not some dreadful imagined state conjured again by hunger and isolation, for I have already found this brutalising. If this were merely an elaborate symptom before some final stage of demise, then I would call on death to take me fast and not tease in this cruel way.

It is partly the generous care and the sustenance I am receiving from this unknown party that causes me to question the truth of the situation. For why have I still not met with the hand that tilts my head towards the tea and the soup bowl, the hand that caresses my ugly damaged scalp, the hands that wash my thin blue body? Why would anyone help such a wretch? And so, have I conjured it all? Do I hallucinate my recovery? What hellish disease might that be?

Uncertain again of what is real, distress returns quickly. When I was part of society I was sure of everything! I rarely questioned anything. What an idiot! Perhaps that is why I am in this predicament. But I was young and busy, busy and young. Oh, but I would so much like to be young again. Just like that again. I would do anything to feel sure of things once more. I don't care about the contradiction. Feeling so troubled is surely not right for a man my age, and perhaps not right for a man of any age. Well, it won't help to be sentimental. At least I am alive. And were it not for recent acts of kindness that might not be the case.

I assume, since I cannot explain it otherwise, that this kindness is that of the shapeshifter. Must be. The shapeshifter taking human form. Certainly it takes on the female form. I base this on the lightness of touch and a human scent, a human scent that seems familiar, a natural, subtle, feminine smell. Not a perfume smell, something more delicate, something beautiful. But beyond that I can still only say that I have a sense of nothing more than the shadowy outline of a figure, the proportions of which seem reasonably consistent with a human being. And I feel relieved. It seems ungrateful to have a preference, but if the shapeshifter took some other form just now I think I would find it distressing, disarming at least, and my resilience has been tested enough. I would really rather not have to deal with anything that might be a shock or make me afraid.

Perhaps I only imagine that the person is female, out of a desire to be cared for by a woman and not by a man, but why? I ought to be grateful for anyone at all taking the time and energy to bother about a man in such a foul state. But you cannot hide your wishes and desires, not from yourself. It might well be Lightfoot who helps me, and though I resist this idea, a part of me feels that I have to entertain it as a possibility. Still, the scent does not lend that way, and the tread of the one who tends me, though it is soft, is really not as light as his. His is imperceptible. Almost.

I can only hope that my situation is truly what it seems, that the worst is over, for I could not face these things again. Starvation is not my skill. I can neither submit nor overcome it. I cannot recommend it at all, and when I am fully recovered I will do everything I can to avoid it. And more than that, I will climb the highest peaks I know and call out from the top that living as I have is really not the way to go!

But I should keep myself in check. What kind of man would shout from the hilltops of his own hardship and suffering? As if my suffering is worse than that of any other man. Always vanity. I hope my self-pity evaporates as quickly as possible and that it leaves no mark for I sense how easily a sense of bitterness might step in. A bitter heart would soon see the small mouse pedalling on nothing more than an old and rusty bicycle forever. Round and round, some terrible scratching sound and nothing but nothing in view. I had better remain vigilant, try to note how my mind shifts, and replace unpleasant thoughts with better ones.

I have been trying to muster the strength to haul myself as far as the window again, but still it is not quite possible, almost no strength in these arms, and though I managed to move my leg and turn my ankle, my body remains quite leaden. I have to wait.

In winter the snow was helpful in dancing close to the

window to show itself, but the buds on the trees are not quite as obliging. I must not miss the cherry blossom.

2.

I have decided on a plan. This body still refuses to do what bodies do, but my mind now makes a good amount of effort, and little by little the pathways in my head begin to lead somewhere, or perhaps my mind maps itself afresh! Re-mapping! I like that thought, but either way, I feel able to settle to a task, for I am going to outwit the shapeshifter, and I am going to see its face!

If I can manage to gain the assistance of my limbs in this endeavour it will be to great advantage and so I try to encourage them. I test them at reasonable intervals, trying to raise or stretch or turn them, but just now they resist almost entirely. But I will not be beaten. I can see, I can hear, and I believe I am awake and alert now for longer stretches of time. So, somehow, it has to be possible!

Unfortunately, my neck is still rather stiff and rarely willing to permit the movement of my head even from side to side. My arms won't support me, but I am hoping that I might soon persuade them to help me lean up using my elbows. If I could gain that position it would help enormously. I have to meet the person who tends me, I do, for recently this person has also sung to me.

When I first heard the gentle songs, a part of me wondered whether I was imagining them. Such reassuring, comforting tones. Then I wondered if it might be someone else? I have settled to thinking that it is far more likely that it is the same person. Has to be. And again I am certain this is a woman, for I cannot believe a man would sing so gently. Well, these are just details, but my thanks are long overdue, and I would like to know their name.

3.

No one comes. I've tried to maintain a state of readiness, concentrating my mind as much as possible, and though I feel quite sure that I have been alert at around the time of their usual visit (for the light outside suggests as much), it seems no one has come. Not today, not yesterday. Oh dear. I have offended them. I have shown not the slightest gratitude and now I am done for.

I cannot imagine that I should ever show such care to anyone in my life, and certainly not without them being my family or closest ever friend, and yet someone or something has taken to feeding and washing a weak and hopeless man, indeed, to tending to the needs of a total stranger. Mopping up my sickness, and all manner of other unimaginable selfless care. I am so embarrassed. I am so humiliated by my situation. And now I am terrified of always being left alone, never being able to fend for myself, never able to re-join society or make something useful of myself. I weep so much and now my nest is sodden.

Perhaps something has happened, perhaps they have also fallen ill. The shapeshifter has contracted something awful from my dull and diseased form. What wickedness am I capable of even when almost totally inert? What damage do I do? What thanks is that to someone who has given so much to you so freely? I am wretched, truly and unquestionably, wretched.

And how could the kind one know that I have lacked the power to speak? It seems the least of it just now, but if only I had been able to utter a few words of gratitude, or written a brief note of thanks, heaven knows this place is full of paper. Well, if I have caused someone sickness by contagion or perhaps through overwork in caring for a terribly sick man, I suppose my brief words would seem meaningless. Would that I was truly well again and could help them in return.

I howled just now into the sheets, wailing high and strong like a new-born. I wish it was so, and that I could return to the womb, start again.

I grieve for the progress I was making, ready to try again to speak, to make contact with the stranger; a step, I thought, back into the world.

4.

Have I slept? Is this night still the same one, the next? I cannot measure. But I feel warm, rather, I feel warmed. It's strange, and very comfortable, I am 'comfortable' in my skin, and just now I moved my neck and head with some ease. Movements in miniature as though I learn them anew, perfectly conscious of them, perfectly aware.

There is something next to me and I delight in being able to manoeuvre well enough to check it out. A row of small black trays, and delicate foods within. They look so pretty. I smell pickled plum. There is water also. And now I realise there is a blanket over me again. A new one. And these sheets, if I am not mistaken, are also new, fresh at least. My stomach hurt just now from laughing! But what a relief!

I thought I had been abandoned.

There is this strange slippage that seems to occur. One moment I am entirely sure of my ability to remain awake, the next I appear to have been in deep slumber, so deep that someone has managed to clean me up and change my nest as well as having delivered me a feast in miniature without my knowing. If I wasn't so cheerful just now all of this would trouble me. But truly, this is such a relief.

What a fool I was to so easily become forlorn and think the worst like that. But I suppose I am entirely dependent, and that is not an easy position to be in, particularly with a stranger. My mother would be most upset with me having accepted so much kindness when I have deserved none, given none; and furthermore would be furious that I have not even begun to offer thanks. Such shame. Well, as soon as I can put things right, I shall.

No closer to witnessing this kind one, I find it disconcerting, it is as though my desire to see them renders them all the more elusive. Is it just coincidence that I do not see them? For it is certainly strange that so much activity occurred straight after my greatest period of clarity and alertness, and that during all this activity I have not once set eyes on them. Not felt a thing. It drugs me? Medicates me? Certainly. But why? Perhaps I exhausted myself with too much animated thought, perhaps I am not as aware as I believe. I had better take things steadily. I have to recover my strength and movement, there is so much to do: fresh planning, the prototypes, the boxes themselves, repairs, and I must check on Cello. It kills me to think of her stored away in a cupboard. I know this was to prevent me from playing, and I know that this meant that she was safe when the typhoon swept through, but still, it isn't right. And where, oh where, is Cat? Does he come and go as he used to? Perhaps he has a new companion. I would not blame him. But if he would still visit at times I would like that.

Lying beside this row of beautiful dishes I feel so indulged, as though I am someone special, and nothing but nothing could be further from the truth. But I will be so happy when I have the opportunity to thank the one who helps me, to introduce them to Cat and to Cello...

5.

The shapeshifter is deeply committed to protecting its identity, for why else hasn't it made itself known? There is never more than a trace image, and the only reasonable conclusion is that it evades me intentionally. Well, alright then. But why? *Why?*

At semi-lucid moments I have definitely heard its tread, but I can't identify it. I have glimpsed sometimes an outline, but nothing more. Perhaps temple staff, one of those who helped bring in the futon and the various provisions. But my instincts tell me not. Instincts. Listen to me! Instincts? It is a very long time since my mind felt quite so agile. The signals, until very recently, have felt entirely lost! As though I couldn't access the right frequency, as though I was denied the means; as though I could not tune in ... to myself. Something not firing, something coming undone, the wiring, the self-wiring, a lack of re-wiring, of re-routing, of maintenance, or the signal box unmanned? Messages, questions, ideas, memories, perhaps *all, all of them*, thrown away, lost in the fetid landfill of the subconscious, in boxes, marked and unmarked, perhaps wrongly marked, mislaid, decomposing, then, suddenly, encountering stimulus, refiguring, re-animating, shooting back, finding a messenger, a trigger, an old one, a different one, creating new pathways, making the way back a way forward. I really do not know – *But Cat is here!* It has been some time, my friend! Nonchalant, he moves his head to raise his chin and looks at me. He stretches long. I envy his movements. The ease of them. He checks out the room, sniffing at this and that and then at the air. He takes in the window, clambers about. He moves towards the steps and heads back to the floor below. A gentle patter of paws.

I can still only conclude for the moment, that if the caregiver eludes me so well, then it has to be a deliberate act. It might be a case of shyness, of humility, or even something more curious, and without knowing, perhaps I ought to remain respectful of this, curb my interest and leave it be. It's none of my business. I am the recipient of the most tremendous kindness, it is the least I can do to act with some degree of sensitivity and respect towards my benefactor. In that case, they will no longer need to hide their face, for I will hide my eyes. *I hear something. The shapeshifter comes!* If I pull the sheet over my face that might be best, then my visitor can relax.

I feel a tension in my chest just now, the anticipation of company, the knowledge that the visitor is to all intents and purposes a friend. I breathe deeply; I have to be calm. My face entirely covered, I keep myself still as though I am sleeping, in that way if they are truly shy or nervous, I will not startle them. I hear neat and tiny steps now as the last of the stairs are climbed, and the house croons warmly that the visitor is most welcome.

Realising that they are now quite inside this room I found I have just had to restrain myself from uttering a greeting and from bowing my head, and now I am almost laughing at my stupidity, but if I am not careful I will surely choke.

I hear the tiny trays of food as they are gathered up. Empty by now, finally I ate all. The cover is now partially lifted, though not by me. My head is being touched, I hear a voice. It is certainly a woman's voice. I sigh happily inside. She speaks with the assumption that I am sleeping. It seems she is pleased with my progress. I am doing rather well. It is quite a change in me that I have eaten and not vomited (*I have still been sick!?*), and that I have managed to feed myself. The sheet is now drawn back from my face and out of respect I have kept my eyes shut tight. I feel my colour rise and wonder if it can be noticed. You cannot imagine what it feels like to be so greatly praised merely for staying alive. In all my life I don't think I was ever praised so highly for doing so very little. I like this feeling. Now my head is tilted and I am given water. I am not sure if I should try to speak. When the woman speaks it's as though she finds me not entirely awake, not fully conscious, and certainly she assumes that I will not comprehend. She talks with complete ease, entirely to herself. I like this also. It makes me feel as though I have access to her private thoughts. Am I bad? I am sure she would speak less freely if she knew that I am actually quite alert just now. The only exception to her assumption is when she encourages me to wake enough that I might drink, or when she is cooing me, as she does now, but even that is done in the manner assumed when someone is very sick and when, most likely, they are not terribly aware of what goes on. But I am seriously glad that I am finally sufficiently conscious to enjoy this experience.

Of course it must also have been wonderful (and certainly it was incredibly kind) that this took place when I was truly sick, but of the times I can recall it was only in some minor and momentary sense, whereas now I feel it as a prolonged and full experience and it is truly blissful.

I keep myself as still as possible that she is not aware that I am now completely awake and fully understand.

She says that though she is pleased by various signs of progress she is worried about my mind; she hopes that I may still make a full recovery. She pauses and then adds that she believes it is entirely possible but thinks there is still some way to go. She needs to see some signs that my mind is active, and she intends to work on this when I begin to respond and display a true awareness. She hopes to be able to pay me visits with greater regularity in order to achieve this. This is thoroughly exciting! I am eager to talk to her, but I remain silent and completely still.

By now I am dying to show her the boxes and the prototypes and explain my plans for them. I suppose I want to impress her. I want to explain how I intend to work on the cardboard dwellings, and the next stage in my plans, how I want these to be clever and dynamic dwellings that might be adapted to all kinds of situations. But for now I do not utter a word, not even a sound, I don't know why ... *but that's a lie*. I know why more clearly than I know anything. I want to lay here with her soft hand upon my head, hearing only the sound of her sweet voice, and her ideas for me uttered in that wonderfully warm and round and caring tone. I can't tell you how amazing this is after all I have suffered, all that I have been through. I am selfish and wretched, I know. I take advantage, but only for now, for just this brief time. I lay in my nest and wrestle away my conscience. I drift into a heavy sleep as though I have drunk the night long on my favourite beer, my head caressed so tenderly. And I feel ... truly drunk just now ... on life.

6.

It seems that I have wrestled my conscience away quite well, for each day, having taken good note of the woman's visits (which now rarely seem to waver), I have positioned myself in my cotton nest and arranged myself in a way that suggests my still weakened state. I do not speak at all, and when she tries, as she has begun most recently, to elicit a response, I give none. And this is easily explained, but it is important to note that it is not some perverted desire of mine to be bathed and cared for by a woman when there is no longer need, nor it is my desire to be fed as though she is my slave or servant. Nothing could be further from my mind. I simply don't want her to leave. I don't want her visits to end. That's it.

If she realises that I am already doing well, recovering at a rate faster than she expects, then after just a few more brief visits to check that I am still making progress and have not relapsed, she will certainly cease to come. I like her. That's how it is. And I am not afraid to admit it. Of course it is easy to like a person because they are kind and gentle and so on, and I appreciate these virtues enormously. But there is something more. I like her company, I have come to depend on her visits, and I have fallen for the tender heart she displays towards this stranger. She is immensely intelligent; endlessly, I would say wildly, curious about the world, really she talks about such tremendously interesting things, and I could lie here and listen and listen ... and so, *and so?* I do. And I couldn't bear it if it stopped. I am not that used to being in the company of such a clever person. Yumi was only about as clever as myself. But this woman is really someone special. I can't tell you how painful it has become trying to hold out from speaking with her. But I know that almost as soon as any recovery is revealed it will signify the end. Of course, I am far from being in complete good health, but I am also very far from dying. I could most certainly fend for myself by now, and day by day I continue to progress and get stronger. Spring is here and so the coldness is no longer a threat, and there is really no need for anyone to worry about me or go out of their way, but I cannot give her up! It is entirely ridiculous, I know. She is not mine. She is not mine to give up. But I can't help but feel attached. I am wrong, I know. But I cannot allow myself to think of just how wrong I am or I will be forced to put it right, and I'm not ready to. I'm not going to.

The matter of maintaining the appearance of one who is still far from recovered is not always easy. In fact, it causes me trouble. For in between visits I can no longer simply lie about and rest the day and night through. I am up and about and have been examining the paper prototypes downstairs and have accumulated a considerable pile of fresh notes. I have also begun to refigure the plans for the box house. At first I was easily tired from all the activity but as the days have gone on I have been able to do more and more. But I cannot actually put my plans into action for fear that the woman might look around the other rooms and find the things that I've been working on. It becomes insanely frustrating.

To lie sick for so very long and achieve nothing is utterly crushing. And so the moment you feel the energy rise inside you again, you can barely wait to get on with things, to re-join life, to rediscover all that you used to do, to redefine what you might do, refigure how things might be. So much excitement! And trying to suppress this is increasingly difficult and often very uncomfortable. On top of this, neither can I sneak downstairs and prepare myself a little extra rice or so, again for fear of this being discovered. By now, you see, I am actually needing rather more food than the woman has brought me (though I hasten to add that I am in no way ungrateful). She does not know that I am expending all this energy and now have need of much more sustenance. And then, the most obvious part of all of this is that I must remain entirely vigilant in case Lightfoot or anyone else decides to pay a visit, delivering something, or else checking on the vagrant hiding out in their quake-challenged dwelling.

Sneaking about like this, in a place that has by now become my home, is really becoming stressful, in fact, it is more so since I have begun to recover, but there is no other way. And so, when I anticipate the woman's next visit I have to make sure that my tracks are well covered; that my notes are hidden, that if they were found they would not appear to be especially new (I dirty my feet and walk about on them in the hopes of giving them an aged appearance); flattening out the sheet on the futon that you cannot tell I have taken a brief rest there (and this I do because I have longed so much to lie upon something more comfortable than my nest upstairs); and then I must check the place over, doing my utmost to ensure that it looks just as it did when she left the last time. I can only hope that she does not grow too suspicious of this man who now gains weight and whose skin must surely radiate a healthier glow – still no hair, but that will come soon I expect.

So strange, I fall for a woman I have not met and have not even seen. I might not like her face, and yet I don't believe that's possible.

I know this cannot go on much longer, but just a few more days, I tell myself, for I will hate it when she's gone. How ridiculous I am. Takeo Tanaka, a ridiculous lovesick man. I cover my eyes in shame, but at the same time I smile, I cannot help it, I begin to notice a feeling I have not had for a very long time, for I notice I am happy.

7.

During the woman's last visit, it was clear that she was becoming somewhat frustrated at my lack of improvement and indeed my lack of response in general: I do not move, my eyes do not open, and I do not speak, in fact I seem to register very little awareness at all. She struggles to make sense of this as I eat so well these days. She refuses to be beaten, and has devised some brilliant activities to try and encourage progress. This has included storytelling, and though often I find I easily drift back to sleep, I am won-derfully grateful, and the stories are always the most seamless pathway to dreaming. She has also hung the most beautiful decorations from high up, that they are easily visible as I lie here: delicate cut-out paper creations of cherry blossom and edible springtime plants, and butterflies – they flutter above me as the breeze catches them. But by far the most impressive of these innovations has been the arrangement of various clothing: trousers, shirts, hats, kimonos and fans as though they are in fact people. She seeks to provide me with a sense of community and society, that I should feel I have some company. She talked all the while she arranged them, and for that I am glad, for if I had risen after she had left and simply found these 'figures' gathered all around, I'm sure they would have startled me in the darkness.

As she assembled each one she explained how she hoped the figures would provide some positive stimulus, perhaps towards encouraging me to feel relaxed and comfortable enough to speak; but above all she hoped it would help me find the place less lonely during the times that she is not here, for she had a job to run to, and must guard carefully against losing it or things would really turn quite bad. She wondered, just briefly, that if this were to happen whether she might not end up quite like me. But she would not let her mind rest on such a terrifying thought. Quite right, I thought. Quite right.

I cannot explain just how much I admire her. If I were a young woman tending a sick and spindly man who seems more capable of vomiting than conversation, I would run. Why doesn't she run? Why does she do this? It makes no sense. If nothing else, I imagine I would have become insanely bored by such a man, and caring for him. But then it has also crossed my mind that she ought to have called on someone professional to intervene. Her behaviour, as thoughtful as it is, seems altogether too eccentric to be that of any traditional nurse. And surely a nurse would have alerted someone and had me taken to a hospital. Why hasn't she done that? Made a call and had me taken in? I'm sure she's neither a doctor nor a nurse, for they are generally quite obedient types, they follow rules, don't they? And they would at some stage of my demise have thought to have me taken to a more sanitary place where I might receive direct and particular medical care, special care, tailored to my condition. It has also crossed my mind, that regardless of her profession, she might still have thought to tell someone. Strange. Still, it seems she has certainly got me past the worst of things entirely by herself, medically trained or not. And by now, this really ought to be the homestretch, I can see that, and there wouldn't be any point in alerting anyone. And yet she does not know of my recovery. So her concern should be all the greater. Yes! For she has commented on the time it takes. Is it pure stubbornness that prevents her asking someone for help, alerting the authorities? Has she set herself a task and will see it through at all costs, even if I die? She is much like myself in that regard. I see that. I don't know her reasons, and I don't actually want anyone else involved, any greater intervention, certainly not in any official capacity, and so perhaps that's it, perhaps she is somehow aware of my predicament in a fuller sense. She sees things as they are: as far as she can tell I am a vagrant, a homeless man, a man with no stake in society, no place, no relationships, and no real occupation. Judging by my condition and circumstances it might have seemed like easy detective work. But what is clear is that despite my desperate situation, and my illegal occupation of this dwelling (not to mention any further crimes I may unwittingly be guilty of), she does not turn me in — even if it would mean that I might more readily and conveniently be tended to. I find this both wonderful and beautiful, and yet entirely bizarre, bordering on suspicious. I hope this is not some terribly elaborate scheme. Some strange plan plotted by some shapeshifter come to cause me trouble. Am I lulled into a false sense of security by some demon who now cunningly adopts a comforting form only to trap me in some relentless nightmare later on? For the first time in days I feel my heart again too clearly. It jumps in a way that draws my attention. I reach for breath. The mouse begins to splutter as he falters, his feet barely able to make contact with the pedals. I place my hand upon my chest and hope to calm things. It's not good to carry these thoughts. I don't remember that I ever had such a ridiculously pronounced suspicious streak. What happens to me? It's no good. I sense myself falling, and dark thoughts move in on me.

I am, by now, must be – twenty-six, and yet I feel a shift of some forty years and not merely this matter of months. Forty years, and a life skipped over, not experienced; and evinced by demise not celebrated with stories, the chapters of a life. Again the sensation of a life compressed, a life collapsed in on itself. *It's wholly unfair!*

I have smacked my hand to my mouth. I uttered the last thought aloud. I issued a scream. I also jumped high. I can't answer for it. An eruption. A splitting of voice from soul. I have crouched down so low on the floor now away from the window in the insane hope that no one heard me, that no one looked up. What a fool I am. It pierced. It was something primal. My throat left sore from it. The throat hurts but I am laughing, trying to contain the sound, at the same time, I am crying. From some place deep inside emotions pour.

It is so long since I have heard the sound of my own voice, it is strange to hear it as such a pure scream. I have not heard the sounds I can make, outside my own head, in such a very long time. The sound of the voice that I have long accepted as mine is the one inside my skull. And that voice is quite unlike the one that emits the scream. And yet I know it to be mine.

I had better keep still awhile. No one has come here, but they might. I must try to keep quiet.

I feel a sudden apprehension about my recovery. Utterly strange, for having lain so long, been ill so long, desperate, and in every conceivable sense thrown away, you would expect only to be thrilled to feel well again, but that isn't quite what it feels like. It's rather as though I visit myself, and do not find the guy I was expecting.

I emerge in an altered state, of course, but it's not how I thought it would be. I think back to the boxes, and the coding – my inadequate repair work. Flaws … so many flaws in my labours. Flaws inside flaws, then accidents that seem to work, that move things on, that open things up, that reveal some small but significant detail, a seed for something more. Rarely is there only ever a total falling away, a complete failing. Nothing ever is entirely failed. Is that the case? Something might be damaged, shot through with errors, ridden with defects, but perhaps never can I say a thing simply has no use at all.

Whether a better or a lesser man, I cannot tell. I am altered by the events and circumstance of these past months, and I expect, by some substantial degree. It is simply that I would hope to be a better man. My deepest fear is that my naiveté will find itself replaced by nothing more than suspicion, suspicion and a deep cynicism, and whatever kindness I was capable of may have been overwritten by selfishness and self-obsession. Improvements are one thing, but it is not that useful if I have been through all of this only to come out less than the man I was. It is still close to impossible to alleviate my anxiety. My mood shifts as though it runs the edge of a half moon, about to take flight at one moment, about to plummet at the next. I am going to have to monitor myself as much as possible and make sure to keep myself in check. This has to include my behaviour as regards the woman, and I now refuse to give in to the tempting thought that there is anything underhand in her actions; I think I will truly enter some entropic state if I continue to succumb to a run of suspicious thoughts and mean-minded reasoning.

If only I knew her name, I am sure it is easier to think badly of someone when you don't know them in some usual way. Whilst someone remains in the realm of the stranger it is all too easy to paint them with whatever traces of deviancy you want to. I see this in my own character quite intensely. Bitching about this woman that I do not know. I get a choking sensation. For if she were ceramic, perhaps just a fragile pot, it seems that in a certain moment, I would simply smash her to pieces.

Nothing! I am nothing but a small man, getting smaller. How messed up is it, that rather than reveal my improved condition and begin the lifetime's worth of thanks I owe, I have taken advantage of her incredible good will? It's indefensible. It has to stop! I must thank her, allow her to see what an excellent job she has done. I will show her that I can not only sit up but that I can in fact walk and do most ordinary tasks entirely unaided.

Imagine then, that upon her next visit, she will be greeted by the fruits of her great patience and labour. She will see the strength returned to me, the energy and spirit, *and we will talk and talk and talk*. And then surely we will share a meal as normal people do. It will be a feast, the atmosphere of a very great celebration, a party. And in this happy atmosphere we will forge a friendship at the very least.

8.

Overnight my ambitions have continued to grow, and I know that until she returns again my mind will run on, and truly, I see no reason that once we have shared in some sensible time together, by which I mean: engaged in conversation and in the proper activity of developing the box dwelling to a finished state, for certainly she will be interested in this, why we should not reasonably develop deeper feelings. Then, as I move back into society and take up a position as a normal, moderate member, I expect we will make plans to share our lives together. We will find a house. We will make a house. Who knows, it might be entirely of cardboard. It makes full sense, for she is clearly enamoured with the prototypes, for who else had sheltered them so well and arranged them so beautifully in the room down there? It is possible that I am getting ahead of myself, and it does no good and is not respectful for one person to make all the plans for two, but these will merely be suggestions. If she would prefer to live in a wooden dwelling or concrete, then I am sure I can be flexible.

It is so exciting to permit your mind to draw the map of 'how it might be'. Truly it fills my heart and I am almost drawn to tears.

I question whether the case I make is ridiculous, but I would have to argue that the evidence of this woman's natural care for me is of an unusually altruistic nature, and one that seems full of affection, and every last bit of this has to be factored in. For what kind of person would take such tender and devoted care of someone they do not know? She is not employed in this capacity, for who would be paying her to do this? She is not obliged in any familial sense, and is no friend of mine (and though I have known kindness from friends, the scale of this is far out of the ordinary), neither is she my girlfriend (not yet, at least), *so why, oh why* should she care, unless having happened upon this place and finding me inside, she perhaps took pity in the first instance and later found she had feelings for the silent man? Don't pity and altruism have limits? For certain they do. And so I am sure her care is for reasons other than charity alone. There has also been too great a display of thought and imagination, I would even call it creativity. And so it's clear, it's perfectly clear that she has feelings that are far beyond those of simple caring.

My mind settles again on how much I admire her, and quickly I feel stifled by thoughts of losing her, though I know I've no right.

But I realise now that if I confess what I have done – that I have hidden the true level of recovery from her – she will surely, and rightly, fly into a rage and leave immediately, and even without a display of anger, for certain she will not come back. But I have to do it, I have to tell her everything. My mind moves through the consequences of so much honesty. I have made my lip bleed from biting it. I know that I can take things to extremes; perhaps I miss something, some detail that would permit a partial explanation, some middle way. The consequences arm themselves. My head begins to ache. The burden of guilt. And I don't hit upon the detail that I need.

I don't know how to manage this, how to find a

reasonable route. I think of possible outcomes. The pressure grows inside my head. Haven't I suffered enough? I cannot escape the sense I have of the loss of time, as though I am old, and this feeling that some decades have been sucked out of my life, and that I am left with only the poor remainder. I cannot get it back! I might never recover the level of strength and the passion I once had, and yet this woman cares for me without this. I hear my aunt, she tells me to grow up, to accept what has happened, to do the right and honest thing. But I know that I will misuse this advice, that I will twist the words, I see that. It is entirely with my own interests in mind that I act. I feel a modicum of shame in this, but truly, what sense would there be in having this woman run away? Making her disappointed in me? Making her feel that she helped a selfish and self-indulgent man? A man quite so unworthy. Well, I had better stop. That's far too much honesty already, it swells my brain. If I carry on I will doubtless find myself writing my crimes and all my private thoughts in large print and flying them outside this house for all to see. Thoughts can really tangle a head in knots. Tying it down. Strangling it. Suffocating the life inside. I have decided on a reasonable way forward and that is the route I choose!

In any case, this woman deserves more than to be let down by me at the last moment. I want her to find me to be all the things she deserves me to be. If things go as well as I hope, surely I need never let her down again. She need never know how much I kept back, or for how long. She can find me recovered, for sure. But I can make the recovery appear to be a far more recent event, occurring perhaps in just the last days, then there will be no need of confession, no need of reprimand, there will be no reason to get angry or to reject our friendship, in fact there doesn't need to be any bad feeling at all.

I am very animated now, if I'm not careful she will enter again too quietly and I will be discovered in some celebratory dance, a bamboo hat upon my head. I should try to sleep awhile, and when she next arrives I must appear only to have made a minor improvement. This I will do incrementally over a number of days, slowly revealing a man returning to health at a realistically steady pace.

9.

I didn't expect that she would come back so soon, but literally, just as I laid myself down I sensed her presence, fortunately right now she remains downstairs. She is not as quiet as Lightfoot, but she is small in stature, and she moves about with the precision of a dancer. Things are tidied away down there, and thankfully I had not just gone down there myself. It might not be long before she comes up, so I had better calm my breathing, right now it is heavy enough to hear.

She climbs the stairs. Silence. A too long silence. I lie beneath a sheet. Breathe but quietly, Takeo. Quietly and slow. She moves something, and now I am newly fearful. I remember that I moved one of the bamboo hats. I played around with it, seeing how it felt upon my head. It belongs to one of the figures that she made and I did not put it back. With nothing else to represent the very top of that figure it will now appear headless. What are the chances that she will not notice? A head is missing. I will have to explain it, and then I will confess. There's no point in adding lies to the scene. A head is missing, and the next will be mine. I can barely breathe. I have to come clean. It's always the fine detail that catches people out, and I will just have to take it.

What happens? Stabbed! I am stabbed! My leg! I don't breathe, the pain is crazy. I have opened my eyes but so far cannot see. And I have screamed out so loud I fear I have shaken up this house as though for the very last time. Surely the roof falls in. Such a blinding pain. I catch my breath. It makes no sense. What happened?

My vision starts to clear and I see now, though some measure away from me, the implement, the weapon. Not even a knife. I have been stabbed, hard, in the leg with a chopstick. A chopstick. I have no idea how to describe this pain. Torturous, *insane-makingly* painful. My stomach has gone into spasm and I am infuriated by the sheer humilia-tion of this – finding you have not even been attacked with a true weapon, but only some ordinary domestic tool! Savage! Truly savage! I wish my eyes would more clearly focus that I might make a full assessment of what goes on here. That stabbing was issued with such force, pure sweet madness! If I had not been caught so unawares, I now have strength enough to defend myself, and I would do so! But this surprise attack, so deeply savage in the delivery, has left me nauseous and crippled in pain.

I gather myself, and now I am drawn to wonder whether the attack is over? Is there a second strike to come? More? Am I to be killed?

I have pulled my knees up and find that I am retching. *Takeo Tanaka!* I hear my name called out, firm and loud. It is a voice that I know – not possible – but when finally, my eyes allow themselves reliably to see, they settle on a face.

It is Shizuka, the woman from my office.

10.

When I saw my attacker, the pain was forgotten, and though I was shocked, I was hugely relieved to find that it was Shizuka and not Yumi or any crazed man. But still, and to my surprise, she kept her position, crouched, one foot outstretched, ready to strike me again, perhaps this time with different moves.

When she was sure that I recognised her she rose up and stepped back, and choosing deep tones, she issued the most severe lecture.

It was not the bamboo hat that had given me away. I had been far more careless. Far more. I had left an impression on the futon downstairs, giving away the time I had spent resting there; I had begun to assemble a cardboard dwelling, and had left plenty of evidence of this ... I had also left a trail of cooked rice – exactly how active had I been? I had no memory of this. Added to which, she had gone through my notes – not hidden as well as I had hoped – but truly these are private things and I disliked the idea that she had so easily taken to rummaging, and so, she was quite aware of the remarkable progress I had made – and hidden! And so, the hat was a very minor piece of evidence by comparison. What she found particularly vexing was the fact that I must have been recovering at quite a formidable rate over quite some days, and yet I had allowed her to stay in the dark and worry. I had also lain here as though still entirely incapacitated and terribly ill whilst she troubled herself with ever more complex ideas with which to stimulate and re-fire my mind, my interest in the world, my imagination, anything at all... Like a fool, I interrupted, I uttered only one word, but I should not have. Remarkable, I said, feeling both moved and humbled. She took it that I was mocking her. I was not. But I realised it seemed that way, especially in view of my deceit. I trusted her. Even jabbing me in the leg was a master stroke, it was almost a kind of enlighten-ment to me. I had sunk so deeply into myself, what better way to snap me out! I did not say this. But I shouldn't have said anything. It was clear it would not go well.

After she had stopped speaking we both kept silent. Marking one another, though I soon let my gaze fall. I felt terrible. A great tiredness hit me, and then I felt rather emo-tional, but more than anything I felt a sense of indescribable awkwardness.

My thoughts settled inside themselves again. Shizuka noticed. She said I must be tired out after being scolded like that, but still, I deserved it, and the chopstick attack was probably as big a shock as it was painful. I didn't want her to be sorry, or to retract anything. I felt like shit but I was tired and embarrassed and felt I couldn't trust myself to behave in a reasonable way, or to say something appropriate, and so I kept quiet. I stared at the floor.

Shizuka knelt down close. Just the sound of breathing for a while. Some tension. I swallowed on a dry throat, and coughed awhile. She passed me some water. I took the cup. I held it a moment, observing the liquid, wanting to drink. Then I looked straight into her eyes. So strange to have this kind of contact after so very long. The friend, the cup. My neck tingled and I had to look away. I sipped the water. Nodded my thanks. Put the cup down. I looked at her again, risking the eye-contact, and this time we both started to laugh, and I began to cry. She took me in her arms and held me so gently but close. I could hear my breathing, and for a moment I looked around, thinking it was Cat. He wasn't around. I said I ought to get myself up and perhaps make some tea, and we laughed again.

My sudden retreat into formality was strange, as though this really was my house, my home, and Shizuka a visiting guest. She would rather have a beer in any case, and we ought to celebrate, for no matter how it came about, a sick man was now very much improving, in fact, he was doing rather well; and two good colleagues were becoming aware that their ordinary workplace chatter had in fact been grand preparation for a much greater, much deeper friendship. A true and real friendship. Boxes, I said inwardly. It's all about boxes. Happy fat tears galloped down my cheeks. They were streaked with joy, and sweet.

Shizuka cleansed the wound to my leg. I was embarrassed at this, now in the full knowledge of her identity. Embarrassed in a way I never was before. Strange to think I had laid back and permitted all kinds of intimacy whilst content that we were strangers.

She joked about my skin, that despite my recovery, it was still thin and pale like shoji paper. I smiled at this but I didn't laugh. I wished I looked much better.

After dressing the wound, which I ought to have done myself, Shizuka set out to fetch some beers. We had speculated as to the condition of my stomach, and whether it would be strong enough to cope with alcohol just yet. We agreed that it was surely time to test it.

Almost as soon as she was gone my head set off on a crazed, delusional highway. I wasn't sure if any of this had really happened. Perhaps just parts were real, others imagined? But the wound would smart again, I would place my hand near the dressing, bizarrely finding the pain reassuring, proof enough that things had happened just as I remembered them. I hoped.

I lay myself down again. Stared at the space ahead. There were easily a dozen questions that I wanted answers to, and fast, and I became quite frantic when the idea slashed through my head that she might now, not come back! Still I couldn't reliably measure time, and though I had been attacked, suddenly I questioned, was it really her? Could a shapeshifter adopt a phantom shape that appears as someone I know? Could I have conjured her image whilst some other being moved about this place and tended me? Attacked me? And if it was truly her, what now? Anxiety spliced right through me.

She would return.

She would *not* return.

Once she left the house she would have time to reflect. There were so many reasons for her to be so very angry; and so far I had been let off quite well. By now she would have given it deeper thought, walking and thinking, mulling over my behaviour, and for sure she would take the decision that she wasn't coming back. I rolled around sweating, immune by now to the pain in my leg. Then sounds. The window in the kitchen down below, bottles as they nudged one another, glass upon glass. I breathed. Wiped my face and arms.

I touched my head as though to tidy my hair, still none. I sat up and waited as steadily she climbed the stairs.

Was my leg alright, now? It was, I said. I truly didn't care. She set out some snacks and had brought up cups for the beer. She didn't realise, she didn't know the thoughts that had ridden my head like an ass. We drank. I sipped, just slowly, then taking a gulp, reminded of a taste I had long missed. And we talked. I cannot say of what, it doesn't matter, but it was just as it was in the days when I was the Box Man back in the office, for I remembered now more clearly that we had talked and talked so often, and later we had shared in the food she would at times return with. And everything was easy. That's what I remember. I drank more beer. This is what true friendship is, I thought. That you can talk and talk and talk, you are comfortably engrossed, you feel at rest but sense a simple kind of joy. What a thing. What a very special thing.

But how had she known where I was? How did she find me? My mind shifted back to my monumental list of questions, and my voice now freshly oiled, poured them out. And why did it matter that I had left the office? And just how long had she been taking care of me? *And why?* And was it only her? *Always her?* Were there others? Did anyone see her come and go? Had she seen Cat? Did she know Cello? She did not answer. But sat looking from the window onto the temple grounds below. For a moment she appeared to bear the attitude and shape of Cat. But still the sound of my voice, as the frantic list ran on: *was she still employed at that office?* Had she moved to another job? Was that alright? Was she treated well enough? Why did she enter through the window? And truly, as I asked at the very beginning, how did she know about this place?

She laughed at me, drew nearer, and filled my cup again and again. She would not answer.

Didn't I remember? That I had told her about this place, on the far outskirts of town, and in great detail? Not only that, but I had told her the story again and again, and with some pride – how I'd found myself in this place after some long night of partying with co-workers, how much we drank at bar after bar, how I had stayed on the train drunk, had fallen asleep and long since missed my stop; and, finding myself lost, how I had slept in some falling-down dwelling, and despite its dilapidated state, how I had enjoyed one of the best night's sleep a man could hope for. Then later, when she heard that I had left, she picked up on some gossip … speculation … versions … and then she had her own idea … and finally, finally she came looking. *But why?* After how long? She did not answer, she stroked her arm, tilted her head. She moved closer again. Small pauses filtered into our exchange, and in these I think each of us looked distant, pulling back again with caution, with care.

It seemed she left the company shortly after my own departure, I didn't pry about the circumstances, and for a brief period she had time on her hands. She said she grew curious about trying to find the house. She hadn't truly expected to find me in it, except for the case that I had drunkenly stumbled in once more and taken up residence perhaps again for just the odd night, but my description of the place had intrigued her. I put down my cup and lay back down. I watched the light as it moved over the timbers high up. I would rather believe, and so I do, that she was deliberately seeking me out, and, that she missed me. Why not? And what's so intriguing about some old house that's falling down?

I told her I was surprised that she recognised me. I drew my hand over my head, half expecting to feel my hair returned. Hoping. She dropped her gaze, she said something I couldn't quite catch. The detail didn't seem important.

She smiled.

I moved again, and kneeling up I filled her cup. And she refilled mine. My head was beginning to feel heavy, I must have been quite drunk. I started to say how grateful I was but found myself stuttering, my nose was running and soon I could barely see, my tears, so great, carrying in their weight all my heartfelt thanks and admiration – the words of a drunk guy. She shushed me gently, her hand upon my shoulder. She took the cup from my hand and laid it down. Still kneeling, I dropped forward, my hands stretched long and low, sorry, I said, for all that I have put you through, for all the troubles you have gone to.

After that I must have slept awhile.

Some parts, some aspects, seem to be missing since then – full consciousness memory, how much time elapsed, some hours? …and what might have been said. I guessed it was the beer and then also the adrenaline, too much bliss. When I next came round I moved to sit up, and Shizuka was climbing the stairs. I glanced round sensing that perhaps it was her double. In her hands she held open a large printed scarf. It was cotton, she said, 100%, just what was needed. She would tie it like a bandana about my head, so that I could feel more like myself, more like Takeo.

I told her how I had long imagined that the house was visited by a shapeshifter, that still I wasn't sure. I told her about the comings and goings, the shadowy figures, noises I couldn't readily explain, how it seemed that something feline crept through the window and slept on the shelf. She blushed. She said that she was not a shapeshifter and didn't I remember how agile she was? She had tested out my office box dwelling more than once. I tried to picture the office, to draw out its image in my head: the walls, windows, the desk and what was on it; then the box … but there were glitches, gaps, and I struggled to pull much of it back. Mostly just shadows. Glimpses.

She explained how she had made use of the box when I didn't have the need, that sometimes she had stayed at the office after rowing with her father. And lately she had crept in through the window here for the same reason and slept on the shelf, it really wasn't all that uncomfortable. She didn't enter by the door for fear of being seen, and considered her makeshift bed an intelligent resting place, for no one expects to find a sleeper on a kitchen shelf.

I didn't like to picture any part of what she'd been through. I didn't like the sound of her father either, but I was glad she'd found shelter when she needed it. Strange and wonderful, the atmosphere of this place. I looked up again to the creaky roof. She looked up too.

Once she lost her job, she found that her father's anger deepened, she couldn't be around him, and so the house had been a useful refuge for a while. And then, by the time things smoothed over she found she simply liked the adventure of sneaking in, it was a private room after all. Time passed by, and it seemed she went unnoticed here. But I always seemed to hear something, a trace at least. Didn't I? She finished tying the bandana, it had taken some adjusting.

She paused. Hadn't I guessed her identity by the food that she brought? She was certain it would give her away. Many of the dishes were quite the same as those she'd brought to the office when I was a box man. Didn't it cross my mind? All fevered up, I never worked it out. She cuffed my arm. She said I hadn't wanted to work it out. I asked about the futon, the heater and all the supplies. Lightfoot was behind them. Though that wasn't the name she used.

The monk had wanted to thank the man who had given such a generous donation to the temple, and when he realised my condition he had wanted to help as much as he could without intrusion, for he was sure I had some project here and that I was devoted to its course. *Did he know about the boxes then? Had he seen me working? Had he found the notebooks? Read them?* She said that he had noticed the repair work I had done, and the temple was deeply grateful. I felt uncomfortable at the thought that they had met and spoken. I didn't say.

She worried that I might be getting too tired just now with so much talking. She asked about my health, in a more general sense, to assess how far I had come, how much improved. She knew I was not entirely better; she wondered if now might be the time to see a doctor? A real doctor, and to have real nursing care? I dropped my head. I didn't want that. I didn't want to speak about it, didn't want to think about it. And things were going well, things were on the right side, surely. What need of further intervention?

She moved her head. A minor nod. And silence. I wondered again whether she had thought to involve someone official earlier on? More animated now, she said that it had crossed her mind, but she was cautious without knowing what had happened to me, or what I might have done, or why I had chosen to hide away like that. At the start I did not have this terrible sickness, or the hunger. I suppose I was simply gripped by fear – the very real fear that I was good-for-nothing. I believe I merely slept a lot, though I cannot be sure and now it seems so very long ago.

I didn't ask her anything more. And she let things be. At some point we had moved to the ground floor, but as often was the case, I did not know the moves. Still the blank spaces. Memory, memory, void. A code was forming. Now I found myself curled up on the futon. A blanket over me. You should sleep, she said. She would go back home now but she would return again soon. 'As usual', she added.

As usual. You can't imagine what bliss these words afforded me. Comfort and joy. I surely slept the night through gently smiling.

11.

When I woke it was to find Cello, retrieved from her cupboard. What a welcome sight. Shizuka had set her gently in the alcove with slippers, a mask, and high up, an elaborate headdress. But after we laughed, she thought to let Cello stand alone without adornment for perhaps we were mocking her, and Cello looked most fine when standing just as she was meant to be. I thought the same was true of Shizuka, but I didn't like to say, it might come out wrong. If you seem rude it can be a long road back. And not always possible.

It occurred to me then, the risk I had taken in playing with her kindness. I can't think of another human being who would be so utterly forgiving. In future I would be more careful. Much more. *Still so full of mischief*, I heard my mother's voice inside me, and I pictured her smile. Perhaps I was not much changed at all.

Shizuka called to me, I had a faraway look.

In the long hours I had lain in this place I had often wondered if, like the prototypes, there might be some changes in me, perhaps even some improvements in character. But just now I was humbled.

I gathered some of the boxes I had been working on, I wanted to explain them. And a few of the damaged prototypes also. They looked so elementary, but I liked this, the simple stages, the awkward even clumsy improvements, the experimenting. I told her how I had hoped that through all the things that had befallen me I might have learnt something, that I might even be a prototype myself! That there may still come a better version. She asked if this other version would adopt another name. *She doesn't like my name? My name?* I sounded petulant, my cheeks burned like bright pickled plums.

No, no, she cooed. And as though distracted by thought she stood up in slow even moves, settling herself further away and half in shadow. She paused and stroked her arms as though to soothe something away, and then she began to explain something curious. She told me that she had two names, two distinct versions of herself, and that she had grown accustomed to thinking of these as: 'indoors self' and 'outside self'. *That's magnificent!* I exclaimed. *Prototypes, precursors, and now the emergence of something entirely new to me, something unique: versions of self that depend on the space, the location, the architecture, and perhaps the climate.* Self was suddenly made so complicated again, intriguing – and the effects of environment ... my mind now much too animated. The latter versions of Takeo, it then occurred to me: Takeo Two and *Three*, had certainly emerged in this very particular space, inside this falling down house...

Shizuka was quiet again. I had stopped listening, settling in on myself again. So long cut off from the world, does this have to be the result? A man inside himself? Tuned in, only to himself? A regression. Not *Takeo Three*, but rather: *Minus One*. Did it have to go this way? Might it be the case, that Takeo Three, whilst in some areas improved, had sacrificed functioning tolerably in other important areas. And now of course, my mind had entirely drifted off. It gets worse!

We remained quiet awhile. I couldn't measure for how long. But long. I began in small ways to fidget.

She asked me, and so gently, if I was tired or perhaps I found it hard to concentrate? Yes, I said. At least, I think that's what I said.

We settled to working at the boxes awhile but without speaking. Not awkwardly, or so I felt, but because there really wasn't any need. Our labour was our chatter, our breathing made us warm.

12.

After she left that day I set to wondering what she had meant:

'her indoors self, her outside self...'

She had spoken of having two names, one for each space. I thought of my feet and putting on shoes to leave the house and becoming the Takeo who goes to work or to school or to visit someone and later, returning home, slipping off the shoes, leaving them at the entrance and becoming: 'at home Takeo'. Is that what she meant? Something like that?

And I was drawn to remember a particular day when Yumi had thrown me out barefoot and I was forced to walk the streets of Tokyo in pyjamas all day long. A confusion of inside and outside, so to speak. I managed rather well but I couldn't have coped much longer. That was the beginning of my demise, of my 'falling', the indoors man thrust outside.

When Shizuka returned I asked her what she had meant. Why she had two names. It was not, as I had imagined, that she simply had two versions of her name, or even just two different names, she had two completely separate identities, and belonged in fact, to two quite different worlds. All the time I spent with her and I figured out nothing. Not a thing. Shizuka Sakai, as I knew her, was actually Korean. Her name at home was Chung Ae Kim, and all aspects of life inside the family home were strictly Korean. When she left the house each day she became Shizuka Sakai, and her father insisted that she lived as though she was entirely Japanese whilst outside her family home. She would step over the threshold numerous times each day – inside was Korea, outside was Japan. She had done this all her life, beginning in childhood, right through her school days, accepting it as normal. It was a form of filial obedience in early youth, and later she continued out of respect for her parents. But as time went on she had found herself deeply conflicted.

Losing it, I blasted the air, *why had she agreed, how had she accepted this? What was the point?* I embarrassed her. It wasn't my intention, but nonetheless.

Her father had thought this best, that this system, his system, would cover all possibilities, prevent judgement in each quarter; that it was sometimes complex and difficult to be Korean inside Japan; that ultimately, if she married a Korean man, she would be a Korean wife, and if she married a Japanese man she could be a Japanese wife.

—Could she not simply be herself?

We looked at one another, and if I had had the strength and confidence I would have held her close. But I could not be that bold. Not then. Useless. And in that moment my bandana slipped. Takeo, the fool. I felt a shiver. Someone's voice. Inside my head. The residue, perhaps, of Yumi. But soon gone. Thankful, so *thankful*, I breathed.

Shizuka seemed to smile at me with deep understanding, and small pink rings appeared to each side of her cheeks, as though a brand new version had just emerged. A more definite version, a 'standing taller' version, perhaps, of self.

She had battled with so much, with so very much … wanting to settle with one identity, with a truth, wanting to know: who was 'she'? *This woman or this woman or…?* Struggling to disentangle one from the other. But seemingly always finding as much reason to be Shizuka as Chung Ae. And growing up, at times she had even found it fun to have a secret self.

Perhaps she ought to choose another way, a third way, her own self, and her own name. I grew bolder. Bolder and bolder. And soon we played a lot with this idea. What an exploration! You can't imagine. We dressed in kimonos, we dressed in paper and boxes, used the make-up on our faces, even a little of the ink, and made ourselves over and over so many times, fresh and new. And yes, we drank more beer.

But you cannot play like children all the day long, she said. I might have argued about this, but I did not want to spoil the mood. We cleaned our faces. Gently wiping away the streaks of colour from the face of the other.

It was time, she said. Time for me to consider coming back again, and out into the world. Time to find a place to live, time to find a job again, to re-join society.

Something flowed away from me. The air was thick and hard to breathe. The atmosphere felt sombre now. She was right, of course. Definitely. And I ought to give these things some thought. We tidied things away, folded each kimono neatly, placed powders and inks back in the boxes they belonged to, and she left for the day.

I had important things to consider, that was certainly the case, but there were other things to do just now, and it was clear that these should take precedence. Besides, a man can only have the 'time' word thrust at him so often before he wilts.

There were fresh boxes now under construction. The ultimate work had begun. I straightened my bandana, gave Cello a gentle bow, and set to work.

You have no idea what tremendous joy and consolation there is in work such as this. I had not even begun to plan the new coding let alone apply it, but even the careful work of assembly was gratifying. Immensely so.

Shizuka did not return for several days, and so I continued with the box work, making steady progress. All the while I remained confident that she would come back, and soon, and I viewed her absence as nothing more than an aspect of her complex rehabilitation plan. 'Time' for me to think. Time to 'move on'. I had to learn to fend for myself again, and clearly I could. But I hoped that she was not in any trouble at home – she must have spent so little time there the last months – and I tried to reassure myself that she would come here right away if anything was wrong.

Between the excessive bouts of work, I considered her dilemma: the two identities, the confusion it must cause, the inner turmoil, the stress and then the brilliance even, of pulling this off, as skilled as an actor. I thought also of the fun that she had spoken of. Somehow I liked the notion of the indoors self and outdoors, this coexistence, the versions of a self, whatever they might be. But my friend's situation was complex, complex in the way that is also troublesome, and my mind, as always, too easily distracted. And perhaps too playful.

I looked at the boxes. They seemed trivial suddenly. I had now to abandon all other ideas and work as swiftly as possible on a project entirely for Shizuka.

I proposed to myself the idea that I would make her a unique indoor space – the culture, the nature and identity of which she would later imprint on the place entirely by herself. I would simply, and loosely, construct her very own box. A space of her own.

13.

By the time she returned, the box dwelling, though far from being finished, was ready for her to try. I had worked on it like nothing else.

She listened as I explained it and she seemed to like the concept, but she was also distant, and I liked this less. All this hard work!

But had I decided about leaving yet? Had I given it plenty of thought? I'd had days and days to think it through, to conceive of a plan that might suit me. To consider the future. Alright, she agreed, I was not yet entirely well, not perfectly, but perhaps the remaining work on my recovery would best be achieved back out there in the world.

The remaining work? Am I little more than a project

now myself? I did not speak. I could not. I settled myself on the tatami, a sense of the forlorn making a fog all about me.

But didn't I miss things? Normal things? If I left this place I would have more comfortable surroundings, a hot bath in place of cold bathing. I could go to hot springs to help me revitalise. I liked hot springs a great deal, she had heard me say as much.

I do, I do! I surely must. But does the work I have done here not show vitality enough? And would the world outside permit the occupation I have chosen? And would I be accepted as I now exist? As I am now? But again I did not say a thing.

Somewhat guiltily she feigned interest in the box. But it was too late now and I knew it was not real. I knew she wanted me to be better, she wanted me recovered, she even said she looked forward to me returning to myself. That's what people say. But I was certain *that* Takeo had gone. He no longer existed in a way that could easily be recovered, in a state, or a condition, that could be reassembled. He is something morphed, altered, accelerated, decelerated, hard to say, but he is other, and not the man that was. Less. More. But by some degree, changed.

It is a devastating feeling to think you might disappoint someone, and worse still to think that you yourself might be that disappointment.

I am Takeo. I am a box man. I live in a box inside a box inside a box.

She sat near to me and tried to encourage my leaving. Paper covered my ears. Her own situation, she now stated, wasn't really that important, she hadn't meant to burden me. She thought me too distracted. Too far, in every way, from the world. In order to return to full health, I should realise that I had to get back to normal, to be, and to live, like others, and I should be able to see by now that the time for this had come.

Layers of paper now fully isolated my hearing. I pictured a cocoon. I placed myself inside.

My health, she said, was the biggest priority, and whilst the atmosphere of the temple and temple gardens had played their role, and whilst good food had nourished my body and I had rested well, it was only by returning to society that I would fully be myself.

I picture a paper Takeo blowing in the wind.

She reminds me that I agreed to think all this through, and tells me that I need not be afraid. She will help me.

She has a bag with her. She takes out some things she believes will be useful, she calls them: essentials.

I do not speak.

I stand up, she motions me to follow her, she places a pair of men's shoes by the door – they ought to fit, they are my size. I move my right leg and make as if to try my foot in the first one, but withdraw it while it hovers in the air. Her hand is on my arm, it is gentle, it is meant to reassure. She smiles at me. I cannot smile back.

I will not leave my home.

14.

Some weeks have passed. Without company and with so much work to do, there has been no time to think.

Spring has truly come in all its glory and I watch the blossom as it hangs heavy upon the trees in the temple gardens, its life too short. But I no longer worry that I might be seen. At least not on the temple side. I have not spoken with Lightfoot, but we seem to have caught the other's eye, and have no need of anything more. I wear my bandana, and he shows his fine head. He has his work to do; and these days I try to make the best of the dry conditions to fix what I can inside this place. I find a box of vegetables at my door from time to time, sometimes fruit. Never meat. I would like a little meat, but that won't come from the temple side. It doesn't matter, and I do quite well. These days my culinary skills might even impress my mother.

Having put aside all other box-related projects, I am also proud to announce that I have finally spent some nights sleeping heavily in the box dwelling. I had to sit up and had poured myself into it, so to speak, so as not to damage the walls, but the place has afforded me some comfort. Oh, I have that futon here if I wish, and there is a closet full of blankets. But for the most part I'm not cold at all; and though it is more common to sleep laid down, I find the box offers me quite a different experience of sleep. I cannot say anything very grand about it or make out box sleeping to be a superior experience, I am sure this is not for everyone, and I do not attempt to sound elitist, quite the opposite in truth, I suppose that box sleeping by choice is very eccentric, but speaking purely for myself, I have to say, that it makes me feel at home.

What occurs to me now is that I would still like to make a more complex box dwelling. When earthquakes and tsunami strike, people face such trauma. The sea makes itself tall, wades deep onto the land, taking what it will; and shaken by the ground, homes and lives are lost. It is not just the loss of a lover or the shame of losing a job that ails people, though these things trouble people greatly, and the mind at times so fragile. We withdraw and are lost. What is common to each is the need of a benevolent hand, a place of safety.

I would like to make something useful. I would like to be useful. I would like to make a very fine box dwelling that affords some comfort, and offers some shelter, however temporary, for it is in the immediate aftermath of trauma that a person most needs to feel safe. I know this to be true. The boxes must be collapsible of course, easy to transport, easy to assemble, the cheapest things to make.

I will make all the fine calculations for these whilst sitting in my box. I have my notebook.

There is a knock at the door of this falling down place. I had better move fast, if they knock that hard again my roof might just fall in! Even so, I tread carefully, tools and materials lay strewn about, quite a mess in fact.

The knock is on the shadow side, the street side.

I open it with caution.

There is a woman, she is simply dressed; she bows and offers me a box of food.

The food in the box is Korean.

Afterword

Identity:

In this fiction I make the dance again beneath the skin of a man, this time a Japanese man. I shiver myself inside him, I empty my mind to occupy his. I take him as pre-existing, a full life, all his own. I take his shape and the shapes of his thoughts as though I am *yokai* (a shapeshifter). And I shiver myself then inside the house, inside its walls, its materials, inside its energy as a stage for fiction, inside the possibilities it presents as a dwelling, again as though I am *yokai*, for I wanted to explore both the human and the house, their space, the rhythms and pulse by which they live, by which they breathe, and the state of their being.

This novel started its life as I began to read Kobo Abe's *The Box Man*. I experienced that ecstatic, too rare feeling in discovering a read I would long cherish. In many ways I still do, but it was the first few pages that took my imagination, and soon after my thoughts departed to a book of my own. This was some nine years ago now as I write, and I planned then to write a man and a box of my own design. Abe is a writer I have much admired, as much for his intense imagination as for his literary skill, and the curious reader will find multiple references in this particular work as a celebratory homage to his. Such a reader might also find a web of intricate references to Japanese films, novels and poetry if so inclined, and yet the story is drawn from my own rich and challenging years living in the snow-bound mountains in the north of Japan, my travels throughout the country, and my time later on, living in Setagaya in Tokyo. I consider Japan to be my second home but most deeply, I consider it to be my spiritual home.

Japan, I feel, as I finish the last work on this book just now in 2016, is facing its own fresh challenges, and its youth seem to have largely succumbed to a nervous conservatism. They travel abroad far less than in the post war years, study abroad in fewer numbers, indeed, of late, it is the student populations of China, India, and South Korea that are travelling the farthest and widest, and from Europe it continues to be the German student population that exhibit the greatest spirit of adventure. There seems to be a lack of confidence among the youth of Japan in recent years, an anxiety, and I am curious as to why this is, or whether it is truly the case. Junichiro Tanizaki, author of the widely acclaimed *In Praise of Shadows* and the less widely read fiction *Some Prefer Nettles*, appears to have lived through an earlier, but perhaps similar, crisis of identity, and prior to 'the great earthquake' of 1923, which razed both Tokyo and Yokohama to the ground, his interest certainly lay in otherness, in foreignness, and he flirted most specifically with Western ways and tastes, indulging in what he later appears to have rejected as largely shallow and specious. It seems that the catastrophic effects of the earthquake, and the postquake landscape, tore at something in him, but such is the intensity of the relationship between the elements and nature with the human, at least from my own observations of Japan: the human living in rhythmic, dynamic relation, and respectful awareness of the natural world. And from then on, having experienced the impact and devastation of this earthquake, and at all levels, Tanizaki sought to live the most traditionally Japanese life he could, moving away from Tokyo to the Kansai region of Japan where such traditions were still more widely practised. The translator, Edward G.

Seidensticker comments in his introduction to the Vintage edition of *Some Prefer Nettles* that Tanizaki's post-earthquake novels reveal the notion that Japanese people can only truly find peace by being 'as intensely Japanese as the times will allow', and this idea of being deeply embedded in Japanese culture, or else returning to it, and rediscovering it, is one I find deeply fascinating – in part, and by contrast, because my own relationship with English culture (what is, theoretically, my own culture) often feels tenuous, fragile, and for the most part does not suit me well, and Japanese culture (clearly not my own) seems to offer up a sensibility, an aesthetic, a way of being that I believe I will always fall short of, yet always aspire to and admire. And so what draws my interest is whether a new generation of Japanese people feel similarly to Tanizaki in the 1920s, for is this now their time in history to renegotiate their sense of self, to reacquaint themselves with their own deep, rich, wondrous culture; and is the conservatism that I hint at, truly that? Or is it time for Japan to pull back and celebrate itself and its most admirable qualities and sensibilities? By staying in their own country, are the young people of Japan simply plunging their hands deep into Japanese soil? And what version of 'Japanese' will that be? What shape will it take? What depth of cultural engagement will present conditions allow? When I think of these questions I am aware of the ironies, and of my own sweet contradictions, and the limitations of what any of us might truly know, but the questions are exciting ones, and I am curious to slip inside them, move around them, observing more closely, and more quietly, more gently – in my view, that is as much as a writer can do – we then simply shuffle words about, and wait in hope, for some connection with the reader.

On Writing:

There are moments of difficulty for every writer that lie quite outside the spectrum of challenges offered up by the bare page and the shifty, mischievous, configurations in ink that curl about the page, and these, most often, are quite enough. But I think now of Vladimir Nabokov and his work *The Luzhin Defense*, for despite that particular novel's success in Russia, the book did not meet with an English translation for some thirty-five years, and this because the author would not give in to an editor who called on him to change the world of his novel from chess to music. The editor in question also called on the author to render the main character as a 'demented violinist' in place of the chess-playing genius, Luzhin, and again, Nabokov stood his ground. *My Falling Down House* met with editors along the way who found it too dark, not dark enough, and then, too international… Most likely it is, too dark, not dark enough, and certainly it is international, but like the chess-playing genius, it has its place, and I would no more bleach nor blot out its centre, its heart, than change its skin. I believe this is called integrity.

Jayne Joso

Tokyo & Toulon 2014, 2015, & London 2016

Acknowledgements

I am enormously grateful to everyone at Chisenji Temple, Niigata, Japan; but I am especially thankful for the kindness, wisdom, and patience of Hiromichi Tamura.

I must offer very special thanks to the local residents of Echizenhama, Japan, past and present, for allowing me access to a number of traditional Japanese homes there – at the time of my research all abandoned and in a vulnerable but beautiful state, and permitting me to make my notes and sketches, and also to photograph these private dwellings. Truly, I crawled and walked and peered so deeply, and everyone I encountered was tremendously patient and accepting. My deep thanks also to my dear friend and artist, Hiroki Godengi, in facilitating this and in sharing his knowledge.

I would also like to thank Kanayo Sugiyama, Kioko Tamura, and Setsuko Taguchi, for sharing, over many years by now, their boundless knowledge of Japanese traditions, culture and nature. I thank Entomologist Dr Ben Price, Curator of Odonata and Small Orders, Life Sciences Department, Natural History Museum, London for all the fascinating detail on the anatomy, and life, and indeed, death of the cicada. I thank Professor of Literature Roger Webster for our invaluable conversations on defamiliarization in literature; architect and academic Joerg Rainer Noennig for our ongoing dialogue on space and place, on process, on the need to make and unmake, to mark the paper and remove, delete, erase, and sometimes mark afresh; and the desire, the requirement and the drive, at other times, to leave the space just bare; Professor of Evolutionary Genetics Mark G. Thomas for too many things to mention; and author Imogen Robertson 'on cello'. I am indebted also to the authors Lydia Davis and Marilynne Robinson for their own writing and interviews on the writing process.

Thank you to Gwen Davies, editor at *New Welsh Review* magazine for publishing an early version of the opening to the novel.

My grateful thanks to Bryony Hall at the Society of Authors for contract advice.

To my publisher at Seren, Mick Felton, and all the Seren team, thank you so much for all your enthusiasm and the care you have taken in bringing out *My Falling Down House*; and to my editor, Penny Thomas, I say, thank you for 'seeing', and for plunging your hands deep into the soil...

Huge thanks, of course to all the friends who have supported me emotionally along the way, for you are many, but I ought to mention: June Zhao, Sasha Damjanovski, Lynne Dragovich, Ian Kelly, Glenda Norquay and Roger Webster.

With regard to the cover, a great deal of love and thought went into this by everyone at Seren. Finally, the wonderful figurative painter Carl Randall stepped in and very generously permitted us to use his work. Thank you so very much, Carl. Takeo could not have a finer coat. Carl Randall's work is frequently exhibited worldwide, and can be viewed online at www.carlrandall.com.

Cent 23·02 22

MY FALLING DOWN HOUSE

And finally, this book was inspired in part by a young man I once knew simply as Takeo, a man I met in London; and another, older man, that I knew as Mr Tanaka, in Gejo, Niigata, Japan. If ever either of you read this, I give you my thanks, and have celebrated you both in the use of your names.